Schelling Point

Achim Littlepage

December 14, 2020

Contents

1

Opening Remarks

IN THE SENATE OF THE UNITED STATES
Monday, November 18, 2030
The select committee met pursuant to notice, at 10:30 a.m., in room 216, Hart
Senate Office Building, Senator John Skinner, chairman, presiding. This
session is closed to the public. Also present: Senators Silva, Reese, Bishop,
Marshall, Golding, Ismay, Sperry, White, Gabrielson.

CHAIR : The hearing will come to order, please. Thank you, my colleagues,
for coming here today. We have a lot to do, a lot to sort through. As
we all know, the re-scheduled general election will be occurring in 8 days.
I will be brief. After my short opening statement, we will hear from a
series of witnesses. Each has responded to a request to come forward and
answer our questions. I commend the patriotic and bipartisan efforts that
members of the committee have made thus far, and I hope we continue
the good-faith efforts. This session is closed to the public, for two reasons.
First, there is a worry that the performative nature of Senate hearings can
take precedence over true fact-finding. Second, we may ask witnesses to
answer questions with delicate answers, and we would like the witnesses
to answer freely. When the hearing concludes, we will make a summary
report available to the general public.

At this point, we have heard many accounts of the events that were set in
motion on Tuesday November 5th. What had been a healthy, if not spirited
and vigorously prosecuted exercise in the democratic process was disrupted
by anonymous cowards. Our faith in the institution of democracy, which
lies at the spiritual core of our nation, was called into question.

Most of us awoke that Tuesday morning to learn that a polling center in Virginia had been bombed. While we, each of us, through our own network of friends and information sources, tried to learn the truth, we were bombarded with misleading information. Text messages were sent to millions of Americans claiming the election had been canceled. Misleading news stories indicated that there were "bombings in polling places across the nation." Weaponized memes spread like wildfire over social media with misleading images, suggesting mass causalities. Several precincts were canceled even before opening. There were reports, false and misleading, of riots and arrests, even martial law. There were reports of voter registration information being corrupted and legitimate voters being turned away and even arrested at polling places. Deliberately misinformative advertisements were aired, suggesting that voters "do the right thing and stay home today." As a result, it became clear that there was no hope of holding a legitimate and untainted election. At 2:00 pm Eastern Time, for the first time in over 250 years, the national election was decreed postponed. As we know now, there was but a single act of terror - if you even want to call it that - a poorly improvised pipe bomb, detonated at 5 a.m., in the basement of a church. This was in the early hours of the morning, before dawn, before anyone had entered the building, in a polling place in Virginia. There was nobody in the building, no casualties. No arrests were made that day. Nobody has been charged with a violent crime. But somehow, pandemonium created by misinformation won the day.

In the days following, disturbing new information emerged from the blockchain world. Smart contracts monetizing the spread of misinformation seemed to be the catalyst, but the terrorists who created these remain unknown, as do their motivations. We're here today try to understand what happened.

We've requested that the witnesses be open and non-technical whenever possible. It is to the discretion of the committee as to whether witnesses are required to swear in. As we feel that good-faith fact-finding is crucial, we will, without objections, be waiving the swearing in for these hearings.

A member of each party has been appointed for the questioning : Ranking

Member Silva and Senator Reese will each be allowed unlimited time to interview the witnesses and may request intermissions. Senators Silva and Reese will alternate questioning the witnesses first.

Again, this hearing is not televised or broadcasted.

2

TESTIMONY OF THE FIRST WITNESS. Mr. Paul Preston, CEO, EWD Consultants, LLC.

CHAIR : We begin by recognizing Senator Reese.

REESE : Mr. Preston, thank you for appearing here. Can you begin by telling us what EWD does?

PRESTON : Thank you Senator Reese, I'm honored and humbled to be here. EWD is a software development firm that oversees the development of cryptocurrency protocols and software.

REESE : Which cryptocurrencies does your firm support?

PRESTON : Tapcoin is the most well-known and broadly used, but we also support Alice, CZZ, and RIZ, actually dozens of lesser-known projects that I won't list. Also, there are a few others under development.

REESE : OK, so to begin. We'd like to discuss the so-called "Bounties" application, which was instrumental in financially incentivizing some of the actors causing the chaos. Perhaps you could give us an overview and maybe a bit of the history of this application leading up to the recent election?

PRESTON : Yes, thank you, I'd be happy to provide as much information as you would like. In fact I'm very happy to be here, to have the wonderful opportunity to share some of the progress that we have been making at EWD. Can you believe it's my first time I've been here? There has been tremendous progress in the cryptocurrency sphere, and I really think it's important that lawmakers like yourselves stay abreast of it. Those of you who know me know that I'm always excited to explain blockchain, because

9

it's such an exciting and dynamic subject, and still very much in it's infancy. It's changing the world for the better. I don't want anybody to be afraid of it, fear is a big problem. I've been told I'm a good ambassador for this space, so again, I appreciate the opportunity to give you guys (and gals, sorry) the inside scoop into what's going on. But yes, Bounties. Bounties is an innovative and economically natural application that is revitalizing the economy throughout the world. We at EWD are quite proud of Bounties and believe very strongly that Bounties is perhaps our most fundamental economic innovation. Bounties has spurred broad economic activity and generated prosperity throughout the globe, now being instrumental in the employment of over 1 billion people. To give a bit of the history, about 8 years ago when we were building the third layer of the Ricci Protocol, we had a vision for Bounties, and made the decision to hard-code the Bounties functionality directly into the protocol, because we believed resolutely that this would be the killer app. We wanted everyone to be able to use it, and be able to use it out of the box. While we are, in general, often reluctant to include more than the basic functionality into the decentralized protocol specification, to avoid bloat and all, this particular one was important.

REESE : I'm sorry, for the benefit of myself, and I'm sure a few others, could you please describe the relationship of EWD to the Ricci protocol and these various cryptocurrencies?

PRESTON : Yes, thanks for asking. I know this can be a bit daunting if you're trying to learn about this for the first time. Ricci is the name of the larger ecosystem, which encompasses a number of permissionless decentralized networks, and the applications built on these blockchains, each of which use protocols that were developed for the Ricci ecosystem. The predominant blockchain is the ground layer for Alice, which is necessary for the stablecoin Tapcoin, which you are probably familiar with. The protocol is a way of communicating and agreeing, more or less. You can think about Internet - which is really just a protocol which allows computers from different parts of the world to talk to each other. The world wide web is a layer on top of the underlying internet protocol.

REESE : Permissionless? Could you, um -

PRESTON : All of the blockchains we develop are by default permissionless, meaning that anyone with access to the internet and wants to participate in the protocol, they can run the software, they can make transactions and they can stake to verify transactions. Basically, it's as open as the internet is open. Anybody can use it. There is no central authority gatekeeping the protocol.

REESE : Thank you, please go ahead.

PRESTON : We, and when I say "we" I usually mean EWD, we develop and code the protocol itself. We have mathematicians, economists, and game theorists designing, tweaking and constantly battle-testing the protocols. Once specifications for the protocols are designed, usually by the mathematicians and economists, the developers implement these, and then we turn it over to the public to build on. Much of our work is writing academic papers which are peer-reviewed. This is the bottom level of the pyramid. Our product is state-of-the-art and rock solid. We've built everything from bedrock to be as secure as theoretically possible. We have some of the world's best coders writing software in a strongly-typed programming language that we developed in-house about 10 years ago. The code supplies a mathematical proof of correctness, so the software is guaranteed to run exactly as the mathematicians and economists specify it. So you're not going to get some of these embarrassing fails that we've seen over the last 10-15 years on blockchains built by duct-tape-and-WD-40, move-fast-and-break-things development teams. The software we create interfaces with the Alice blockchain, which is essentially just an extremely long condensed list of every transaction that's ever happened, and some other programming instructions thrown in. This is real money. Our protocol is behind about $25 Trillion in assets. So we think long and hard about our protocols. We don't own the network itself, the network is necessarily decentralized. But part of the consensus of the network is the agreement that we all use the same protocol. If not, the network would be useless. Now once we've specified and developed the protocol, other application developers, or just end-users can interface with the blockchain by using the protocol. For many applications, we just wait and encourage developers to build their own layer. But for the Bounties -

REESE : I'm sorry - maybe go back a bit, can you define a little bit more what you mean by "the network" here and describe, if you can, your protocol?

PRESTON : Yes, good questions. So think about the word wide web. It's just millions of computers. No one says when you can log on or log off - it's basically open and decentralized. You have to get a provider, but all your provider does is connect to other computers on the internet. The important thing is that in order to function, all of the computers on the internet have to be talking the same language in order to communicate with each other. This isn't automatic. I can't just plug my computer into the wall and just expect to have it speak computer to its friends, all the computers have to be taught to speak the same language. The internet protocol is constantly updated and improved by a number of different organizations. Now for blockchain, the protocol is an agreed upon method for deciding who gets to say what goes on the chain. The network is simply all of the people who choose to participate in this blockchain, using this protocol. Again, a blockchain is literally an ordered list of transactions. Every potential transaction is cryptographically signed, so you can't fake a transaction, you can't forge it - I mean, I can't create a transaction with your money if you don't give me your secret keys. The worst thing I can do is to try to create an invalid transaction with my own funds. The most obvious reason why a transaction would be invalid is that it's incompatible with a previous transaction, most likely because that money has already been transacted and sent somewhere else. So that's why the chain has to have a particular order, otherwise we would have what's called the double-spend problem and the whole thing wouldn't work. I hope this makes sense. I spend a coin by signing a transaction giving you that coin, and you confirming that the transaction made it onto the chain. If the transaction is added onto the chain, necessarily it didn't conflict with any previous transactions. Now that I've sent you the coin, you get to spend it, by signing a transaction with your own secret key. And because there's a transaction back there which says I gave it to you, it now belongs to you, of course, until you send it elsewhere.

REESE : Perhaps you could explain this a bit more, how do you sign with a secret key?

PRESTON : Right. Blockchains are based on public-key-private-key pairs. I will avoid the temptation to dive into number theory, but basically there's two huge numbers which we call keys. One is private, known only to you, the other is public, known to everybody, and everybody knows it's yours. One number can be used to encrypt a message. The other number can then be used to decrypt it. And vice versa. So I can write a message I want to sign, and encrypt it with my secret key. With my public key, anyone can decrypt the message. Now if I didn't encrypt it with my secret key, and you try to decrypt it with my public key it won't work, you get garbage. These keys work in pairs. Technically, you need to use a hashing function - encrypt a transaction with one number using the hashing function, and decrypt it with the other number. A hashing function basically takes something legible and a big number and mixes these together into some gibberish in a way that is essentially impossible to reverse, without knowing the other key. So using your public key anybody can check to see if a transaction was encrypted, or "signed" by your private key. It's like 500 digits long so no one would ever guess it and it would take centuries for a supercomputer to cycle through all the possibilities to find it.

REESE : Great, thank you, this makes sense. Signing a transaction is like signing a check. This double-spend issue is when you overdraft?

PRESTON : Uh, not to go too far into the weeds here, but usually you have to refer to the transaction that gave you the coins in order to spend it. You can only do this once, if you don't spend it all you are creating a new transaction that you refer to later when you want to spend the balance.

REESE : So the double-spend issue is when you sign two valid transactions referring to the same transaction?

PRESTON : Exactly. Very good. The solution to this problem, the basic idea of

Satoshi, was a protocol which forced everyone to do massive computations in order to add the next piece, so that the blocks are created in a nice steady order. Because the process of verifying the validity of a certain transaction is fairly easy for a computer to do, you have to create competition in order to decide who gets to add to the chain. In Proof of Work, which is what Satoshi devised, you have this competition, and the winner gets to write the next block and gets a reward for writing it. That's how new Bitcoins were created and this is often called mining. As we all know by now, Proof of Work is insanely wasteful and inefficient, because it simply requires computers to burn electricity at an unheard-of rate. Everyone my age and younger, OK, not everyone, but, yeah, everyone believes in global warming, by now, so burning carbon sources for no reason is not something most people are eager to be associated with. It's incumbent upon all of us to develop and support more efficient uses of our resources. So we developed a protocol called Delegated Proof of Stake which cuts out the mining aspect and replaces it with a lottery. I don't want to go into all the possible attacks here, but the main thing is to make sure that people who are likely to not help the network function should not be allowed to participate in verifying the transactions. With Proof of Stake, your chances in the lottery are determined by how much of the coin you own. If you own a significant piece of coin, you probably get to write blocks, but you are less likely to be malicious and hold back transactions or do other things that would muck around with the effectiveness of the network. If you want to do any serious damage to the payment network, you have to own 51% of the coins to start with, or hope for some string-of-atoms-in-the-galaxy sequence of improbable events.

REESE : OK, so I'm not 100% sure I get the motivations in all this, but, perhaps we'll come back to that if it's important. But if I understand you correctly, your corporation created a protocol so that the network can process transactions?

PRESTON : Yes, this would be one way to sum it up. We created a protocol that efficiently decided who gets to add the next transaction to the blockchain. It's a good protocol, so billions of people have agreed to use it.

REESE : OK, so you oversee the Bounties project? Please continue with the history of this project.

PRESTON : Yes. We were very excited about this project, going many years back. Once you've thought about blockchain technology for awhile you see that it allows all sorts of fascinating pieces of the free market to come play together. It took years for many people to see this, but the Bounties project was something that was more or less clear to many of us as something that needed to be on our road-map. The gig economy has been booming for the last 15 years or so, and we wanted this product to dovetail with the needs of the gig economy. The vision is that, basically, you want to be able to outsource any task, and have it done in a reliable way, by someone, somewhere around the globe. We all have learned that we don't need every task performed by someone taking up office space. Some tasks are easily and more cheaply done by some brilliant and hard working kid in India, who wasn't lucky enough to be born in the Silicon Valley and isn't paying $15000 a month in rent.

There were a number of very basic platforms allowing workers to find gig work, but it was always somewhat complicated, and the intermediary was always bound by incredibly burdensome regulations and as a result, these intermediaries had to take a huge cut to make it profitable. Of course, they take more than they need to be profitable, but sometimes they are taking 30 to 35% even sometimes up to 70% of the cut. The gig economy had been growing in popularity but it was sort of monopolized by the few apps that serviced this market and these groups were taking a huge cut. These startups (I don't need to name them) had huge private equity backing and like 10 years of runway to be non-profitable. So our goal was to dis-intermediate these entities, and put the whole gig economy on a decentralized network. That way anyone could use it, and there would be no regulatory compliance issues and the profits would go directly into the economy. If we dis-intermediate the intermediaries, we make everything more efficient throughout the globe. So we were working towards this when we first built the foundations for Ricci, because it's such an essential, fundamental tool. There was a lot to do to actually get this to work. There were a number of other coin projects that tried to do something like this, and some of them raised billions of dollars, but the "move fast and break things" motto doesn't work so well with blockchain. You can't afford to fuck it up, pardon my French. We spent 3 years working out the game theory, and then another 18 months specifying the product and another 24 months implementing the code. Over 40 academic papers, published and presented at conferences. We even invented our own blockchain programming language, based on Haskell, because we wanted the code to be mathematically correct and provably true 100% to the specifications. So the protocol is rock solid. It's robust. It's metastable. We've proved that the optimal strategy of players coincides with a Nash equilibrium. We've had papers accepted to dozens of conferences in Computer Science and several journals in Economics. So after five or so years, when we updated the Ricci protocol to include Bounties transactions, we were very excited and very confident. This was maybe 6 years ago.

REESE : So Bounties was originally designed as a tool for the gig economy?

PRESTON : The gig economy, yes, and also the market for computing power, mostly in machine learning. We designed it for both purposes at the same time. I guess the gig economy aspect is obvious, but we also saw this as way to sell computer cycles, or perhaps computer cycles combined with a little clever programming ingenuity. What we thought would be the killer application for this protocol would be delegated machine learning tasks: In particular, given an objective functional, there would be a bounty to find better model parameters that beat the previous benchmark by a fixed amount. We actually believed this would essentially challenge Panigal Web Services. No one really bit, at least at first, for some reason and we couldn't figure this out. Marketing is tough. I guess this is what happens when you build a tech company stocked only with hard science researchers and not so much market researchers.

REESE : I'm sorry, maybe this term is important, I'm trying to stay with you. Object functional?

PRESTON : So in machine learning, you would like to take trillions of data points and use this to build a model that predicts an outcome, given some information about a new datum coming in. We have ways of testing to see if a model does well, if it minimizes the "loss", that is, if it minimizes how often and how badly the predictions fail to be correct, when evaluated on historical data.

REESE : Also, the term "model", you mean like a formula, like $e = mc^2$?

PRESTON : Good question. Sort of like this, but there's a lot of constants, a lot of parameters that you can throw into a model, and rarely physical intuition. Models start with a certain structure, and you try to find parameters that fit the data. "Model" is a funny term in that it doesn't necessarily suggest that you are respecting any physical laws, like assuming something is following a heat diffusion process, but "model" in some cases can mean a big black box that inputs parameters and independent variables - these independent variables we usually call "features", and then outputs the dependent variable, which we call the "target". You change the parameters if you don't like how the model is performing. Classic example, if you have a bunch of two-dimensional data you would like to get your y value corresponding to your x value. The simplest model is a linear model, which requires 2 parameters, you know, y = mx+b. The parameters are m and b, the input (or feature) is x and the output (or target) is y. So you play with the slope of the line m, and the intercept b, until you are happy with how well your line fits whatever data you have.

The goal is to find a model with loss (this is the objective functional) as close to zero as possible. The formula for the loss can be specified precisely, so that anyone can tell if they've beat a certain benchmark. For example in the line above, you typically aren't going to have data landing right on the line, so your loss will be simply the sum of the squares of the differences between the actual y and the y your model gives you.

Now fitting a line is easy to do. Any computer built after 1975 can do this quickly. But when you're dealing with nonlinear models, trillions of points at a time, it becomes a difficult problem. You may now have millions of parameters. In fact, you can have as many parameters as you want, you can make your model as complicated as you like, which leads to the problem of over-fitting. Over-fitting means you have so many parameters that you are able to sort of cram your model into some strange and unnatural function that happens to match the data, but doesn't generalize well. It matches well for the past data, but the next point you feed the model might output garbage. The solution to this typically in industry is to test a model against some data which you have held back and use only for testing. However, it would be very inefficient or impossible in a decentralized ecosystem to set up validation against hidden data, so you have to compare the model against easily available public data. The point is you want people to know if they've beaten the benchmark without giving them the validation data. So what you have to do is include in the objective not only a measure of how far off the predictions are but also what's called a regularization term. This term quantifies how complicated your model is. Back to the 2-d data, suppose you want something more complicated than $y = mx + b$, which is simple, not that accurate, but can actually be useful but maybe not useful enough. Then you can try to fit this to a quadratic, this gives three parameters of flexibility, you know $y = ax^2 + bx + c$, and so forth. Or if you're modeling epidemiology or something you can try a logistic curve with 3 parameters. Now suppose I give you 10,000 points in a plane. You're right, I could come up with a 10,000 degree polynomial that could fit this perfectly, but this would be garbage - it wouldn't generalize well to new data. In this particular example, you could add a penalty for each parameter you use - this way you are encouraged to choose a simpler model. It won't be an exact fit, but we wouldn't expect that anyways. If you can find a 4th degree polynomial that fits the data well, go with that, that's great. You want to balance between a simple model and an accurate model, the assumption being that simple models are more robust and less likely to be distorted by over-fitting. In practice, models are complicated and can have millions of parameters, so to find the best one, you have gazillions and gazillions of different combinations of parameter values to choose from. One of the amazing things about deep learning is that there seems to be a much lower dimensional structure to the way things unfold in our universe and deep learning has an uncanny ability at finding this - so you don't really need the millions of parameters to describe a good model in the end, but to start - you don't really know where to start without them. What you do with machine learning isn't really that complicated, you just plug in some parameters and check the objective functional, then you plug in some slightly different parameters and check to see if the functional is lower. Remember when you were a kid and you tried to figure out the square root of two with a calculator? You try 1.5 times 1.5 and that's too big. So you try 1.4 times 1.4 and that's too small. So you try 1.42 times 1.42. OK I was a bit of a nerdy kid - it's possible you didn't do this - but this sort of iterative process is how some kids approximate the square root of 2 up to several digits. But with machine learning models it's far far more complicated. Instead of just measuring how far your square is from 2, you are measuring how far the predictions over the entire data set are from the ground truth values. The error is the loss function. If the function has been lowered, you move to that particular parameter value and start looking around again for better parameters. When you have parameters in a very high dimensional space, it takes a long time to search for other parameters, because there's so many combinations of variations. This is often called the "curse of dimensionality". A ten by ten grid contains 100 points, a ten by ten by ten cube lattice in 3-dimensional space contains 1000 points, but if you have, even twenty parameters, a grid with 10 divisions for each parameter is going to give 10 with 20 zeros after it - number of points. Often you just want to check the value of a function on all these points to find the best one. But once you get into the millions of parameters this is impossible. Lowering the objective functional means that you found some parameters that are slightly better, more general, more accurate. Usually this takes some combination of brute force, computational strength and some clever programming beyond just vanilla gradient descent. But after the initial cleverness and a little tweaking, mostly brute force computation. The idea we had was that you could farm this out all over the world, instantly pay whoever gives you a better model, and continue paying people, perhaps upping the bounty, using auctions or other marketplace mechanisms until you have a really strong model, very accurate but also very simple. And anyone could do this - you don't have be Tapboard or Panigal to have access to this sort of supercomputing power.

Unfortunately, the adoption was slow out of the gate, at least slower than we had expected. Neither the gig type bounties nor the machine learning bounties seemed to receive a lot of attention. At the time we didn't really fit in - we were not really a classic tech firm, nor were we one of these hardcore Bitcoin maximalist crypto-anarchist ideological outfits that seem to generate excitement and fandom in the crypto industry. We build everything on science and our understanding of what's necessary in the market. Obviously this paid big dividends down the road, but seven years ago we didn't have a lot of traction.

REESE : OK. So I think I'm following. You see a market opportunity - create a market for doing these large computations. Maybe someone can do these computations in a clever way. You want to incentivize this. But you're saying this wasn't recognized immediately as a useful tool?

PRESTON : Right. Our marketing wasn't great. We decided we wanted to kickstart the project a bit. There were a lot of centralized competitors. These competitors usually paid people in fiat and used more of a ham-fisted verification process, but I guess people were happy with it and didn't want to switch. Even though the gig economy was booming, we found that we had a lot of trouble with the buy-in. It was tough to compete with the legacy systems that were charging 30% fees, even though this is highway robbery. Unfortunately, around the world, like I said, the reception was kind of, meh. You have to build the network effect. We had gotten so much interest in the years leading up to launch. Perhaps it took us too long to develop it, I don't know. Anyways, we had the idea, which I still think was a touch of marketing brilliance on our part, to market Bounties to college students who wanted help completing their homework and term papers. You asked for the history, right? I knew we were going to be getting a lot of grief for this. However, philosophically, we believed that in a decentralized network, you can balance the rewards for doing something one shouldn't be doing with the danger of getting caught in an economic way. It sounds bizarre if you're trained in the mindset that government is the only entity that can fix things, but it works great. The problem (and this goes for a lot of things) is that when the enforcement of certain rules are centralized, they are prone to fail, by either good old-fashioned corruption or just lack of attention. But, if the enforcement is decentralized, it will work well, provided that the incentives are set up properly. So we had set up this system that allows students to pay anonymous people online to write term papers for them. What we did was floated the word out to college students that you could offer someone, you know, $4 to do your homework for you, and someone would. So a few students made these offers, and we actually, for the first week, had Ph.Ds here at EWD doing freshman calculus and biology homework for $4. Not a great rate, also ethically-touchy people might say unethical, but it had the desired effect. After a couple weeks, a number of other freelancers joined in, as did hundreds, then thousands of students, and then after about a month, there were about 500,000 requests on the network for this type of service. Of course this is going to be abused, if by abused you mean people are simply paying others to earn their degrees. But we had imagined a different feature of this network, which allows for a sort of decentralized sting operation, and is designed to catch people who abuse the system to cheat. Now university administrators aren't idiots, and they screamed foul. Everybody screamed foul. This story made it into a lot of mainstream media like the New York Times, if you remember. But we had a solution, the free market will always provide. You see, decentralization and anonymity are always double-edged swords. We were able to give universities the tools to more or less inject, with some probability, a number of, at least from the students' perspective, adversarial actors into the system. This was all free market in action. The university would put out a bounty, created in a way so that these double agents could insert something into someone's homework assignment, and you could identify this coded snippet in sort of a secret, cryptographic way to the university, then the university would pay these adversarial actors a bounty. To bust you.

REESE : - so the universities were running sting operations on their own students?

PRESTON : If you want to call it that. I mean c'mon, you guys in intelligence do this all the time, am I right? You have to keep the game free -what's good for the goose is good for the gander. But the universities at first were furious, they thought this was immoral or unethical or something. But they adapt. All they had to do was inject a few adversarial actors, and raise the penalties for getting caught. The universities weren't happy that they had to do anything, but it was quite easy to find a service that would snag the students - we had this ready to go. The universities still were mad, they came after us, and were really angry that they had to resort to this, they were all like "urhhggh, we uh, don't condone these, uh, sting operations on own students, this is morally reprehensible." There were a number of lawsuits, but these lawsuits didn't go anywhere because, basically you can't sue a protocol, and it's not like this is the first time in history students got their term papers off of a website - what it was the first time for, was an opportunity for universities to actually catch the students, and have cryptographic proof that they did this. Once we showed them how easy it was to thwart the cheating students, they started catching students, imposing penalties and the whole thing dried up within a couple weeks. Yep. They were OK with it. Professors were absolutely delighted - for years, cheating, you know student conduct panels had always been just a "he said she said" thing and professors often felt like they would go through tons of paperwork that didn't lead to anything with any sort of a bite. But now we have a cryptographic proof and then it's a slam dunk. I've received literally thousands of emails from professors thanking me for this tool. They all want to remain anonymous because they don't like to be seen celebrating this sort of thing in the PC academic culture, but secretly, professors love this. They really do. So when all was said and done, everyone knew about Bounties, as we had hoped, and started using Bounties for all the other things. Nothing like the media gorging themselves on a scandal for free marketing, right?

REESE : If I'm understanding this, the solution to online plagiarism is to have university administrators pose as freelancers on a sting operation?

PRESTON : No, no. Not the administrators. It was much easier than that. The university uses a protocol we had ready to go - right out of the box - for this very purpose. A student wants you to write a term paper on Critical Race Theory and they want to pay you $20 for this. So the freelancer (who is also probably some dude in India) writes the paper, then hashes a piece of it, with a code provided by the university, along with his or her address, and posts this to a network. Then they send it back to the student. The university can then run hashes of some predetermined piece of the paper, and compare it to what the freelancer hashed, and confirm that the student did not write the paper. It's easy to see which universities were participating, so once a given university put up one such notice, word spread fast and all of the students stopped using the protocol to cheat. It was beautiful to watch.

REESE : OK, that doesn't sound easy to me, I have to admit, but I'll take your word for it, this sounds a bit daunting. Not to get too far off track, however, I do have a feeling my next question might be relevant to some of our later discussions. I don't think I understand how a paper that someone paid, say $20 for would be judged as a reasonable paper. How does this verification happen on a decentralized network by anonymous participants?

PRESTON : Sure. Another great innovation. In the thousands of Ph.D hours we spent designing the game theory, we came a up with a system such that the validators are incentivized to provide honest answers, and when applicable, accurate answers to basic questions. The basics of this go way back - we had futures markets like Sooth a decade ago which laid the groundwork. Basically, if you ask 1000 people a question, and the answer is obvious, and they get paid for giving the consensus answer, most people will just choose the obvious answer. You know, like Family Feud. You try to guess the most common answer. If there's one true answer, that's obviously the most common. Now if some subset has incentive to lie, the solution is simple, (actually, the details are not simple) but in essence, you just have to decentralize this enough and combine this with a rarely used backstop process in case things get really wacky. For example, we could ask who won the Super Bowl, last January. While I'm sure you all in this room had the 49ers, you would give the correct answer of the

Patriots if you were all to answer simultaneously in order to settle a bet. Now maybe half of you did bet, and decided to collude and agree ahead of time that when the question came up, you would answer "the 49ers", this would work against you if we simply extend the poll to a larger pool. For example, I could randomly text 5,000 people from around the US and tell them they get $5 to text me right back who won the Super Bowl - I'm going to get the right answer overall. Especially if I build in disincentives. So there's a network, tens of thousands of validators, that just validate things continuously and get paid in small increments to do it correctly. I hear it pays reasonably well, and makes a good supplement to people with part-time work from the gig economy. If you start supplying wrong answers, the system knows and you lose your stake and have to work your way back into the system. So the incentive is always to provide correct answers to questions. The backstop if a group lies about the Super Bowl is that this can be challenged, and goes to a bigger pool and requires double the bond, large penalty for lying. This can repeat if necessary. For things like term papers, it wasn't so much a yes-no answer, but was this term paper a good paper? complete garbage? so we had to develop what we call "Phidelity" - it turns out there can be a remarkably good consensus as to what an "A" term paper is and what a "B" paper is, and what a failing paper is. The validators are incentivized to improve Phidelity scores, basically, they should all try to agree, without communicating, as a way of forcing themselves to be consistent over time. It's amazing - consensus did emerge. There's now a somewhat universally accepted standard for say a B paper in a 300 level sociology class at a quality school. Funny thing, the "A" papers weren't the most expensive. The free market determined that "B" papers were the most expensive. Students wanted a "B" paper so as to not raise any red flags. If only they knew how predictable this is.

REESE : So I think I follow. Somebody puts out a request, for a say a "B" paper on Nelson Mandela and then someone sends a paper back to the requester, and this paper is verified by the validators, who basically grade it, for a small fee.

PRESTON : Exactly. There's some parameters that can be tuned, like the requester can reject the paper if it's judged too close to A or if 10% of validators thinks it's failing. There's a lot of options.

REESE : Now from what I've read thus far, this Bounties coin, (or Bounties app?) was used in the election shenanigans, right?

PRESTON : Yes. It's not a coin, it's basically an application layer, by the way, but I'm happy to talk about that. But I do want to linger on my previous point just to give some background about where we were coming from. We have always firmly believed that we are creating more solutions than we are problems, and this has guided and framed our response towards much that has happened. So when we first started noticing a pattern of weird activity on Bounties we didn't think much of it, or that is, we didn't think that anything too mischievous was going to come of it. We definitely saw some bounties that looked strange, perhaps illegal, perhaps unethical, inappropriate, untoward, offensive, whatever, but we never have once taken this to governmental authorities, mostly as a matter of principle. The ability of humans, both individually and collectively, to correct for problems arising in systems of behavior is almost always underestimated. Every time in the past, and there were many times in the past, when it looked like someone was using our network for some antisocial purpose, it usually just played itself out and fixed itself. Occasionally we would give a free market nudge, not-so-much a nudge but pointing in the right direction, for example, by showing the universities how to catch the cheating students, but usually this all just played out nicely in a laissez-faire manner. We first had some serious discussions during the 2028 election. There was a lot of pressure at the time to step up and say something, do something. Someone, maybe a foreign actor, maybe not, was paying image engineers to download pictures from pretty much every predominantly white neighborhood in the country, and carefully paste in videos or images of what appeared to be Somalians and Mexicans involved in some sort of drug deals or gang rituals, or even, like, human trafficking. The end goal was for these to be posted on Tapboard Locals, so the quality had to be decent enough to get by Tapboard's deepfake filters (which isn't saying much). These were quite extensive - there was even a short video set in front of my house posted in my Locals. This video, at least according to the caption, was of a Somalian drug lord meeting with a Mexican and apparently passing drugs for distribution, and there was a blond girl in one their cars who seemed to be in some sort of distress. Now I knew this was bullshit immediately - I've never seen a Somalian within 50 miles of my house, and while there's probably 20 Mexicans in my zip code, I'm on a first name basis with all of them, and can say with some degree of certainty that none of them are selling hard drugs for Somalian drug lords or kidnapping Scandinavian girls. This was quite a trip to see going down in front of my house, according to the video, but I guess someone just wanted to spend some money to stir up racial tensions. I think it worked in some parts of the country. Anyways, we thought this was definitely not a pro-social use of our product, but after a number of discussions we decided to not make any sort of official statement or position. Our product wasn't essential - we were providing the marketplace but not much else. We left our employees (some of whom were quite fired up) to feel free to contact authorities about this - I believe some of them did, it's none of our business at EWD, they just weren't supposed to do this as an envoy of EWD, but I think some employees intended to try to actively speak out against this, in particular, to lobby Tapboard to do something to stop spreading these altered videos. Of course, Tapboard could give a rat's ass, they like to keep racial tensions piping hot as long as it drives attention to their apps. There was a lot of fuss and hand-wringing going into the election but I think this was sort of forgotten about shortly after the election, as all of the hyperventilating media found something else to get worked up about. I don't think this played a role in the presidential election, although there are some people whining that these did have an effect in some liberal leaning white suburbs who suddenly found themselves electing a conservative representative who's a hard-ass on immigration. I don't know. But this was the worst of the previous election cycle. And this was a presidential election, so we expected much worse. But it actually wasn't too long after the start of 2029 that the strange Bounties first appeared - and they seemed really odd at times and also very brazenly suspicious. Like there was a large bounty, several million dollars, for anyone who could produce the source code to the voting software used in a few select precincts. This seemed really strange. It was never fulfilled. We didn't report this to the FBI or anything, because we figured they could see this - and we were right - they asked us what we knew almost immediately after it was posted. And again the bounty never resolved as fulfilled. As far as I know the FBI could've posted it themselves. Who knows. People are always asking for illegal stuff, but usually it goes nowhere, it's just a waste of time and a waste of about fifty cents, or fifty cents and putting $1 million on escrow for a month. We can't waste our time with it.

REESE : And what did you tell them? The FBI, when they asked?

PRESTON : We convened a very quick meeting and decided unanimously that we weren't going to break from company policy. We aren't jurisdictionally a US entity, as we're not incorporated in the US. We had already had a number of discussions in the previous cycle and were pretty much settled on our policy. Now we actually didn't have any information - we had some evidence that whoever this was had always used VPNs or TOR or something, so we wouldn't have been able to tell the FBI anything more than anybody else on the network, but we didn't even want to tell them that. So we told the FBI, you know, good luck figuring this out, but basically this has always been our stance on how we respond to these things. In this situation you have to keep a consistent policy, as lack of willingness to provide information about a specific case can be information itself unless you do this on principle. So we keep it simple. Draw the line once and not every time. No information to authorities unless compelled by a court order, which we typically would appeal, by the way. Now that was our policy, and as you might notice I'm sort of diverging from that right now. After some discussion with other stakeholders, I'm OK with being open in this setting. This isn't a secret FBI subpoena, it's a Senate hearing. This doesn't mean that I'll be answering every random request about every teenager trying to make a quick buck selling a Sparkle kit over the internet.

REESE : We appreciate this. If you could, could you tell us a bit more about some of the bounties that came to your attention?

PRESTON : Some caught our attention but weren't really that sinister, and others were concerning. In the less sinister category, there was a series of identical bounties that basically drafted several people from each congressional district, and then paid signature gatherers to get them on the ballot. This was in every single Senate and House race. Whoever created this had a bunch of money laying around, and they called this project "Real People" the idea was to have an unaffiliated non-politician on the ballot for every single race. These were literally average Joe's, like your uncle Joe people. People applied and were hand-selected by somebody, and then there were very generous bounties paid to signature gatherers, like $1 million to gather enough signatures, per candidate. This whole project cost perhaps a billion dollars and was successful in it's stated goal in that every single national race had someone on the ballot that seemed like more or less some random dude. But with a billion dollars spent on this project, and the funny thing is, no campaign funds, no campaign, no advertising, just getting their names on the ballot. I suppose it's totally legit way to spend your money if you have billions to spend to put a bunch of random people who will never win in the race for Senate, but, y'know, fine, OK. That caught our attention because in the end, like nobody even knew who these people were. Anyways. There were a number of other more concerning ones - for example the request looking for dossiers on all of the precinct chairs. Slightly strange, at the time, but amongst the sea of requests people are making for information, especially in the political arena, not too crazy. These seemed to escalate, as then there were requests for lists of precinct chairs' family members' names, which caught our attention because the request was so brazen in what it was looking for. A lot of this information isn't hard to find, and in fact most of the bounties were paying, I guess, a fair market price for the information. Many times it was just, compile a dossier answering these 25 questions on so-and-so, and the payment would be $300-500. What was bizarre is that some of these requests were quite large. There was a $3 Million request for a full dossier on someone who owned a pizza shop in Bloomington, Indiana. No reason whatsoever given, just several explicit questions. Apparently a lot of the students knew this guy, but didn't know much about his background, and apparently, no one ever figured out the answer to these questions. I guess a number of students actually quit school and tried to discover these answers, but failed. Crazy story, but certainly not the the only crazy story. My guess had always been that this was probably going to be used for social engineering purposes.

REESE : Social Engineering?

PRESTON : So it turns out, and this may come as a big surprise to those of you who think computer hackers are a bunch of oddball neck-beards who speak binary, but much of hacking is done by personal persuasion. You can't crack a password. You just can't these days. But what you can do, is figure out a bit of information about someone, and try a few possible human weak spots. For example you can port someone's SIM from their actual phone to some phone you just picked up, provided you can give a convincing story to Verizon. I know some people who do this for sport, and it's a piece of cake. The more information you have about someone, the easier it is to get control of their devices. So it seemed there was some groups out there accumulating information on people who had something to do with the election, What crossed our mind was that the voting apps used to certify the election must use some sort of two-factor authentication, and some without bio-keys. We had noticed a trend in targets related to the election, but there was also a whole bunch of people who didn't seem to have anything to do with it. And this was not restricted to any geographic place - it seemed like it was all over the country. We didn't know exactly what they were after, especially as the number of requests grew.

REESE : So did you ever think about reporting any of this to the FBI?

PRESTON : We revisited this occasionally, but always had the same questions: Do we draw an arbitrary line and say, OK, 3500 strange requests is when we will suddenly start being part of law enforcement? And the answer was always no. We also didn't know exactly how to report, because we didn't really know what the interests of all the actors were: because there were thousands, I don't know which ones are part of this attack because they seemed to blend in with other requests - requests to provide evidence that so-and-so is cheating on his husband or whatever. Now we have always encouraged law enforcement to use the same tools available to everyone else on the network, unfortunately, law enforcement has generally been skeptical of our methods, although these methods would make a great tool. Maybe there's some laws against using our tools to obtain convictions, not that this has stopped law enforcement before. I also want to emphasize that we shouldn't really have had to report this, because every request that came in was happening in front of the public as much as it was in front of us. That's the nature of a public request. It wasn't like it came across my desk and I had to stamp it. It's an open decentralized network. It was reported by a number of media outlets - not the, you know, mainstream ones, but a number of journalistic organizations, both on the left and the right, were keeping tabs on this with great excitement. I think some people eventually got bored because in the end these requests just became statistics that didn't seem to come with any sort of coherent narrative. We assumed that law enforcement was paying attention. Now I think you probably want a full account of what has happened over the last few months, and to be honest, I don't have a lot to tell you, other than we just supported the ecosystem and let things play out. This was all public. That's the point of a public, decentralized blockchain: there's no God's view that lets us see things that others can't. So we were surprised as you guys were, I'm sorry, as you ladies and gentlemen were, to see that not only did the abuse appear to affect the election, but that it caught law enforcement flat-footed. We really expected that nothing would come of these strange requests but a number of arrests. Instead, as we saw, we had all of this criminal harassment of election officials, and strangely, no arrests so far.

REESE : OK, let's get into some more specifics. Before the week of the election, there were approximately 15,000 bounties for personal information - dossier and doxxing requests, and then 2,000 requests that were identified as "hacking bounties" and over 500,000 social media bounties for a number of purposes. Who was creating these bounties?

PRESTON : We don't know, and we don't, as a general practice, make an effort to figure it out. The term being thrown around is "guerrilla marketing." There are several guerrila marketing firms, and the serious ones, and I assume serious people are behind this, they would be using TOR or other mechanisms to disguise their identities. So short answer, we don't know. We don't have gatekeeping privileges to the network, so our information that we have isn't special. Now, longer answer, you probably have been briefed by other agencies based on the same information that we have, that these statistically fall into certain business hours of operation of certain countries. I don't know if this means anything - I mean it could be a deliberate false flag. The fact that a cluster of the bounties came in during hours 8-6 in North Korea and also 8-6 in Iran could mean that it's people from China or just a bunch of crazy night-owls in Alabama. Read into it what you like.

REESE : OK. Talk us through election day. According to the timeline, the first alarming activity started to occur in the early morning on Tuesday November 5th. Let's start with the text messages.

PRESTON : Yes. I remember Tuesday morning well, it was my 40th birthday. I had been looking forward to celebrating, thinking that our day would be non-eventful. I got a text from one of my coworkers early, that there was a bizarre bounty. This bounty first showed up about 7 a.m. Eastern Time. The bounty paid to send automated text messages to blocks of phone numbers throughout the US. In these phone numbers were embedded validator numbers, this was so the validator could verify that the message had been sent. Also some of these contained photos with QR overlays. I'm not sure exactly what the laws say about falsifying text message information, I don't think it's hard to do, but I'm pretty sure it's illegal to give people false information to deliberately screw with elections. So whoever ended up taking on these bounties was probably in some country far away, Nigeria or India or somewhere, and had access to SMS-spoofing technology. They sent tens of thousands of texts all over the country, saying that the election had been canceled and included links to a fake news site. They also included information that if the QR-overlayed memes were widely spread, whoever posted the memes would be getting paid well.

REESE : And how much did they get paid?

PRESTON : About $10 million. This was the group sending out the texts. There was another $10 million in escrow for paying the memespreaders. I believe it was one organization who accepted the bounty. Typically they may use different addresses to collect the proceeds, but it all seemed to be the same organization. We have no idea who.

REESE : Is there any known affiliations with the individual or individuals who had created these bounties?

PRESTON : I don't know explicitly, although whoever placed the bounty seems to have tested the waters beforehand, and tried this with a smaller scope and more unremarkable text messages. About a week before, they had tested this by putting out a bounty asking for mass SMS unsolicited advertising of some ED drug. This was much smaller, about $10,000.

REESE : Now some of these text messages directed people to a website on the darkweb, is there any sort of luck in determining who put this website up?

PRESTON : Most people couldn't get there anyways. Some people with the darkweb access immediately started reposting the content, took some screenshots, and the host site crashed very soon after and then went dark completely. The memes that were spreading all had QR overlays and seemed to bump right up to the top of Tapboard's algos. The point was simply to spread some poison, and that worked. Enough people were curious and also, confused about what was going on. A lot of older people have no idea what the darkweb is and why this website was blocked by their provider - which led to confusion. As we see now, that was the entire point.

REESE : After the initial texting spree, these disinformation memes continued to spread widely over social media, in particular, Tapboard. How was this accomplished?

PRESTON : So for sometime leading up to the election, large groups of people who are willing to share content for a fee were recruited. This was a bounty itself. Basically, the way this works was if the Tapboard user shared content, they would receive some small amount, anywhere from 3 cents to several dollars in most cases, but in some strange cases much higher. Most of it was anodyne, the content, that is. But it had been going on for a while, and these people were Pavlov-Skinner conditioned to just share this content that was shared by certain groups - the impressive part was that the fee they got appeared to be random - so you really had a bunch of Skinner's rats running around. Sometimes people would get $20 for two seconds of work, other times it would be five cents. Psychologically, this is hard to resist. Everybody expected this was to just spread the usual partisan garbage we see slung around social media every election cycle that everybody cries foul about. This happened two years ago, and it was just sort of forgettable. In my opinion these meme wars are just sounds bouncing around echo chambers in most cases and just people barking at the wind in other cases. The total effect is nil. So we pay no attention to it. Not worth my time. This year was different because the information being shared was distinctly not overtly partisan, and was being shared by people on all sides of the political spectrum. If your crazy survivalist racist uncle on one side and your commie Marxist niece on the other are sharing the same information, you're at least curious. This is what happened. First, there was a massive amount of money spent encouraging people to share some memes saying there was a bombing, and sharing the news link to the local news outlet that broke the news. Then immediately, there's a flow of hysterical posts claiming that the election had been canceled, sharing pictures of bombings that didn't exists, there were all these pictures of random backpacks. This is where whoever did this used some great choreography - next came a wave of reports that the media had completely contrived this story - there was no bombing, that some ulterior force was out there spreading lies about a fake bombing. I admit, I actually fell for this briefly, in the sense that it struck me as something that could be essentially true, that maybe a pipe had burst in a church and the media was trying to scare us again, like they always do. We all know the media can get whipped into a hysterical frenzy over nothing at all. So that's what I figured, and that's the narrative that was promoted very early by the these bounties. But as the morning went on, people started to realize that no, the bombing was real, and whoever was posting claiming the bombing was false was obviously getting bad information. Then the reports start to escalate again. What made this so effective was that it was based on truth. It was indisputable that there was at least one bombing. This was all over the news. But whoever did this had a real stroke of genius in swinging this back and forth, so people really didn't know which way was up and who to trust. Now this was all early in the morning. Then of course, this "manifesto" or whatever it was gets posted on the Bitcoin blockchain, accidentally or not, no one can really tell, but people are reposting links to the transaction containing what appears to be this manifesto and claiming that all sorts of people are going to get blown to bits. Now the process is the same - people are pushed a meme, along with a little message, the message saying "please share". Often a group owner will post these memes to the Tapboard group, and if the user's account has a possibility of earning some cash by sharing it, there's a little icon that pops up on the user's panel. Now this is Tapboard, I don't run Tapboard, I only support the currency that is used for these transactions, so I have no idea why this wasn't shut down once it became clear to reasonable people that this was used to deceive people. Ask Scott, I'm sure he will be his usually forthcoming self. This should have been shut down, in my opinion. Tapcoin, which runs on top of Alice, can't be shut down, it's a decentralized currency. But applications that run on Tapboard can be restricted. It's not through a centralized server per se, they like to say that they're decentralized, but this is only partially true. The heavy advertising part that makes all the money and broadcasts and promotes memes can be shut down, while the more organic content which is not promoted by algorithms, that can't easily be shut down. But the spammy engines behind these memes spreading everywhere could have been shut down and in my opinion should have. That's on Scott. I understand you're going to invite him here as well. He could have shut much of this down if he wanted.

Like I said, I don't know much, but I can tell you more about the details that I do know. These bounties are smart contracts, which are really just transactions that can be referenced later by future transactions. If certain conditions are met, the transaction is resolved and funds get sent somewhere. It would get really heavy if you included the entire instructions of every single bounty on the blockchain, so what we came up with when creating this is something called a Merkle Annelid, which is sort of like a side chain. There's a series of nested contracts that can live temporarily on other websites, and once they get resolved, a more compact version exists on the chain, sort of like a historical trace. You can create scripts that create these MA, and they can be pretty complicated nowadays - I mean you can reference a huge database stored somewhere else. Another purpose of these MA is that the smart contracts that require a lot of identity shrouding can be quite heavy - so it's cheapest from a computing perspective to run this as far from the main chain as possible. Sometimes you have to be a clever blockchain engineer to design these things, but it's something a lot of people can do now. Essentially, you don't have to store the entire instructions on the blockchain, you just store resolution points. All the extra business lives on a side chain that is maintained, much like a blockchain, but this gets deleted, or rather, forgotten, lost, once everything is resolved. So when the dossiers of all these election officials where created, there were sidechains holding this information, and the transaction fees were quite high. So there were quite a few of these big bloating side chains with all this information floating around. Whoever it was had created these for people to populate, but there was also, and this was built into the MA, a termination date. These sidechain would cease to be funded November 12, which means that the miners have no incentive to maintain these databases, and no one gets paid anything to act on them. So they essentially vanish. When these dossiers were created, before the election, they were set to terminate November 12, and all of the bizarre markets, which fed into these sidechains, necessarily lasted only until November 12. The contract was built so that it had to resolve by November 12. Most bounties are based on this sort of architecture. We have some built-in templates, but more advanced programmers can be very creative with these.

REESE : So what sort of manpower was behind this operation? Is this something that would require a big team working months on end or could it be accomplished by a lone wolf?

PRESTON : We don't know who did it, but it could have been done by a single person. I say that because while there were thousands of bounties posted, these were basically identical, but with different information. If you know what you're doing this is just liking writing some macros to process data on a big spreadsheet. It really is. You can batch create thousand of scripts, especially if you designed your original dossier correctly. The other aspect of this is that if some parts of the script-writing become tedious, you can easily farm this out. Someone in India will save you 10 hours or work for $50. It easily could have been done by one person. This would have to be a bright person, and would require some planning, but we all know at this point that orchestrating this sort of mischief would involve an above average IQ.

REESE : So since November 12th, have you seen any particularly strange bounties?

PRESTON : Actually, no. We haven't. Well, we've seen a few, but they are sort of random, almost like someone's trying to get attention copycatting the original bounties. We have, however, seen a lot of other activity, in particular, creation of dark MAs. We have no idea what these are doing but we've seen a surge of activity. They are very heavy, and expensive to run, as they use heavy shrouding techniques. There could be a reveal involved. For example in the previous week some dark MAs had been sunlit, and this was how some of the doxxing of precinct officials occurred.

REESE : Can you give us more information on these dark objects?

PRESTON : Typically, you create the MA with temporary databases to store information. When you want to allow anybody and everybody to interact with it, you don't encrypt it. Then anyone can interact with it. But we wanted to have the option to have private MA, by virtue of encryption. So I can do all this stuff I want to on a blockchain, but only people with certain keys or with a password can actually see what's gong on and interact with the chain. This makes logical sense because most enterprise demands this. This way you can have several parties, say corporations and governments, throughout the world, operating on a sidechain for a while in an encrypted way. There's a security issue here in that you can't change the password, so if the password leaks, the whole world can see (modulo some reverse engineering) what's going on on your little sidechain. Typically the solution is to make these temporary with many resolution points. Once a certain set of transactions is complete it gets resolved and disappears. This is incredibly common. As for the MAs created recently, some of these do seem to be more than the standard fare of corporations putting together some sort of escrow deal that they don't need their competitors privy too. I have no idea what, and that's by design. I don't have the MA password, and I'm not on the whitelist. So I can't tell you anything about these chains. There seems to be a lot of them, and they are pretty well funded. At least the escrow accounts appear to have billions of dollars waiting to be spent on something.

REESE : Do you think these pose a threat in the near future?

PRESTON : Honestly, no idea. Not really any good way to tell. Again, a lot of weird inexplicable or unexplained stuff happens all the time on the blockchain. Until it's explained.

REESE : But what I'm more interested in, from someone closer to the network, is some idea of who had access to this kind of Alice or Tapcoin. These request costs hundreds of millions of dollars, all in all, am I not correct?

PRESTON : Yes, you are correct, these request were denominated in tens of millions of Alice which is worth about $12.33 as of this morning, so there was quite a bit of money out there. Now this doesn't tell us too much information on who it could be. We did our ICO at 10 Alice for a penny a few years back, so a smart person who had invested a few thousand dollars in Alice could easily be a millionaire if they chose to hold until recently. A lot of people invested much more than that - I believe we've minted a few billionaires. So if you're trying to use finances as a way of narrowing down the list of suspects, you might have a tough job, just because so many people have become wealthy over the past fifteen years.

REESE : Any idea what whoever did this was looking for?

PRESTON : Again, no idea. Bizarre, sure. Not sure what the motivation is. I don't see an endgame here.

REESE : Are you aware of any heavy hitters that would do this for fun?

PRESTON : Fun? Maybe. It's possible. There's a lot of people who have lots of cryptocurrency that didn't get enough attention from their parents when they were younger. This, this, is something else though, and requires a lot of money to blow.

REESE : Right - so with that criteria - a lot of money to blow - does this narrow it down?

PRESTON : The most socially active whale is a Chinese national who goes by Jing. This doesn't seem like something he would be related to. Jing funds all sort of social justice protests. He funds protests and riots, but usually these have a very distinct social justice warrior flavor. He's been trying to install Marxist regimes throughout the globe. It could be, maybe just an attack on democracy, to show us how much of a joke democracy is. Jing is a big globalist, bigtime communist, hates American values. But that being said, what we saw is not his MO. Maybe one of his students though? I wish I could say more.

REESE : He has students?

PRESTON : Lackeys, wanna-bes. Mostly Chinese but a whole bunch of loser communist antifascists around the globe worship him. I don't know how many are wealthy enough to do anything like this.

REESE : Do you know if any state actors are active participants in the network?

PRESTON : We suspect so, yes.

REESE : Do you care to name any?

PRESTON : Actually, we suspect that most states have been buying coins and staking them.

REESE : North Korea?

PRESTON : I'm pretty sure.

REESE : China.

PRESTON : I'm pretty sure. Quite sure. I mean. C'mon.

REESE : Do you know for a fact?

PRESTON : Yes, well, no. It's just common sense. C'mon. Why would you not have a stake in this - especially if your government isn't burdened by red tape - nothing stopping the parties in power from jumping to nationalize industries or work in their own corner. It would be weird if China was not heavily involved in the network.

REESE : Any hard specifics?

PRESTON : Honestly, no.

REESE : Could a nation state have pulled this off?

PRESTON : Absolutely. That would be my guess - except for I don't know which one. It could easily happen though - if you have a team of sophisticated coders and a bit of a war chest and an ax to grind. It's easy to cover your tracks in this space.

REESE : Do nations leave fingerprints that you can identify?

PRESTON : Yes and that's sort of the weird thing - there aren't any sort of fingerprints that match up with previous operations that appeared to arise as national efforts.

REESE : Is there anything you can add that might give us any insights into who might have done this?

PRESTON : Probably another nation who just wanted to knock us down a bit and had gotten lucky speculating in the cryptocurrency market years ago, and maybe didn't know how to spend it? It could also be some loser who got in really early and hasn't gotten laid. It seems like a lot of work to go through ... but for what reward? Sorry, truly, that I can't tell you more.

REESE : Well thank you for coming in. Thank you for your time. Chairman, I yield my time.

CHAIR : The ranking member is recognized.

SILVA : OK. I will jump right in. You indicated that, and I quote "Jing big globalist, bigtime communist, hates American values." You also suggested that Jing funds social justice actions including protests and is trying to install Marxist governments. Do you have evidence of this?

PRESTON : Everybody knows this - there's a number of videos where the dots have been connected. Jing is a globalist. He pays protesters. Buses them in all the time.

SILVA : Using the Bounties app? I'm learning about this app, just recently. Bounties does at first glance seems like a perfect way to pay protesters.

PRESTON : That's a good point, it probably does happen to some degree, but Jing must be oldschool - he makes payments using other methods.

SILVA : But don't you think this would rule him out? If Jing pays protesters en masse and was behind these disruptive activities which used Bounties, wouldn't Jing use Bounties for paying the protesters?

PRESTON : C'mon. I don't know. Maybe he's just trying to throw off the scent.

SILVA : What do you know about how he pays protesters?

PRESTON : It's in a number of videos. I've posted these on Tapboard. You can watch. I can't remember the details.

SILVA : Really? I've watched these videos. I watched three of them, at least. These guys are crackpots. Total quacks. I'm disappointed, to be frank. You've been going on and on about how academic your organization is, but these videos you cite are conspiracy nuts ranting about nonsense. Certainly you have some evidence to back this up?

PRESTON : I'm sorry. What is this?

SILVA : You told the Senate Committee that there's a very rich Chinese national who is hostile to the United States, who funds activists, installs Marxist governments - I would like to know what you actually know about this guy and his motivations.

To start, how much is this businessperson worth?

PRESTON : Trillions, easy. He was a majority stakeholder in Tapboard - perhaps still is but I think he sold some of it - by the way - I don't know why he would want to mess with Tapboard - it would cost him a bunch of stakeholder value. That would be shooting himself in the foot.

SILVA : Whatever happened, it doesn't seem like preservation of capital was really the goal.

PRESTON : OK, I'll give you that. Jing bought into Tapboard big years ago - the other founder, not Scott, but his cofounder had actually brought more capital to the table when Tapboard was founded, so the other founder, James, I believe his name was, owned about 80%. Apparently James just got fed up with all of Scott's bullshit - I don't blame him - and sold all his bags and split. Jing ended up with like 60% of the equity in Tapboard. But that's trillions right there. He's had a bunch of other trades, an uncanny string of trades. Always seems to time the market right. Before getting in Tapboard I believe he had some stakes in Chinese exchanges which is how he made his first buck. So I've heard.

SILVA : Have you met Jing?

PRESTON : I have not.

SILVA : Have you communicated with him?

PRESTON : I don't have a distinct memory that jumps out at me, but the chances are that yes at some point we may have communicated. We run in some of the same circles.

SILVA : Do you consider Jing a rival? Colleague? How would you describe your relationship to him?

PRESTON : Huh? He's just an investor. I build stuff. We don't really have too much in common.

SILVA : OK, how about Da?

PRESTON : What about Da?

SILVA : What was your relationship to Da?

PRESTON : I'm sorry, these questions are feeling a bit pointed but somehow at the same time unspecific. What do you want to know?

SILVA : You've described a bunch of hearsay and folklore about people in blockchain. I want to know, what you, Paul Preston, know about these people.

PRESTON : I see you've done your homework. I'm-

SILVA : Of course I did my homework. This is a select Senate Committee meeting and I'm talking to a trillionaire who designed the currency that much of the world economy is operating on. This isn't an impromptu AMA. I did indeed do my homework.

PRESTON : I'm feeling a little ambushed here. I thought we were going to talk about Bounties, not every interaction I've had with everybody over the last 15 years. What do you want to know about Da?

SILVA : Do you know anyone who would have wanted him dead? You know he was killed about two weeks before the election, correct?

PRESTON : I'm debating whether to say I know that or not because you'd probably ask me if I held his hand as his last breath left him otherwise how would I know? I was aware through my information channels of this fact, yes.

SILVA : And do you know if someone wanted him dead?

PRESTON : That's a strange question. Considering he was murdered.

SILVA : Very good. Can you tell us any reason why?

PRESTON : Should I not be answering questions here? Like, without my lawyer?

SILVA : You're free to answer or not to answer, we're just trying to get a complete picture of what's going on here. There's evidence, evidence that I'm sure you've seen, that the entities who financed the assassination of Da also financed the attack on the recent election. Da's assassination was a result of a bounty. We're trying to uncover what's going on here.

PRESTON : I'm uneasy with your tone. Am I on trial here? Can I ask you some questions about exactly how you've profited by insider trading over the last 8 years?

SILVA : You're free to go if you like. We really do appreciate that you've taken the time to come in here and explain everything. I've learned a lot. But we're just learning about this character Da, and we'd like to get to know more about him and what sort of enemies he had, or maybe not even enemies, people who would have some interest in seeing him dead. Something he might have known, or some way in which he could have posed a threat. He seems like a complicated individual so we are hoping you could help us out.

PRESTON : Listen, I don't need this right now. It seems like you're just fishing for something, I don't know what. I've had a lot of interactions with Da over the years. We worked together all the time. Now he's dead. I'm not going to enumerate every deal we've been involved in. Did someone put you up to this? Who suggested you interview me? Why am I the first one to take the stand? I'm here voluntarily. Did Scott put you up to this? Did Scott accuse me of something again? Listen, I didn't have a goddamn thing to do with Da's assassination. Perhaps you should save these questions for Scott. Scott has been involved with Da and Jing for quite a lot longer than I have. So you should be asking him. I'm done.

But, I should probably tell you. I wouldn't put this past Scott. He has the resources, and he has that clean hard working Indian thing going on, but he was born and raised in New Jersey, he's cutthroat.

SILVA : So, just to be clear here, as this is not something I want to take lightly. You are suggesting that the CEO of Tapboard, Scott Greywahl, could be behind the assassination of Da?

PRESTON : OK, so I'm just offering speculations here. Sorry. But I should mention that when I first partnered up with Scott to create Tapcoin, I received a series of unsolicited messages telling me that Scott was capable of things that I couldn't imagine, and that if I had a bad feeling at any point, I should trust my gut. I think it was "stick to your guns and moral principles, if you give him an inch he will take advantage and you will soon be doing things you disagree with." I assumed this was from James Andrews. Then he told me that I should never do anything unethical or illegal with Scott, even the smallest thing, because, this email said, he "grooms people like that."

There's been talk, I should add - that Tapboard is hoping to collaborate with the US government in the entire elections process - make it happen all on Tapboard through a giant ledger. I have mixed feelings on that, but I can tell you for sure that Scott would love this. So if you're looking for motivations, think about it - if you want to make the entire election an online blockchain affair, the best way to do that is to create a giant clusterfuck out of the traditional method, like we just saw. But I wouldn't be surprised if this whole hearing is just a sham concocted to come to the inevitable conclusion that we all need to do elections on Scott's social media app already.

SILVA : OK, now we're getting somewhere. Scott Greywahl, who will indeed be testifying soon, the CEO of Tapboard. You are suggesting he could be behind this? You told me a few minutes ago you didn't really know who this could be.

PRESTON : You know, I'm not sure what games you're playing. I'm just talking and I feel like you're just trying to gotcha me but I'm not really sure why because this won't even be on TV, so I don't know who you're showboating for. I'm not really sure what you have against me Senator Silva but frankly you seem like an angry woman and I don't need this right now. I'm out. Have fun with Scott. I hope you get some answers.

Mr. Chairman, am I free to leave?

CHAIR : Mr. Preston, thank you for your time.

3

Sworn Statement of Alan Rice, Fairfax County Sheriff

In the early morning of November 5th, at approximately 5:27 a.m., our offices received a call from an individual in the basement of Our Redeemer Lutheran Church. The rector, who lives in the parsonage, had heard a loud sound, and went towards the church to investigate and noticed that a portion of the brick wall on the east side of the church building was damaged and water was gushing through the wall. The rector indicated a belief that something had caused a pipe to explode, so he had first proceeded to disconnect pressure on the main and proceeded to enter the building to investigate. After finding shrapnel in various parts of the room, and no explanation for the explosion, the rector made the decision to call 911, as well as the local utility board. We arrived with a team and were able to begin investigating. We determined, after a preliminary investigation that an improvised pipe bomb had been placed inside the inner wall on the east side of the church basement. During elections, when a place of worship is the precinct setting, it is often the practice to cover posters or symbols that may manifest any sort of political or religious nature, the goal being that the polling location maintain 100% welcoming atmosphere to citizens of all religions and political persuasions. It appears that a hole had been cut into the wall, the bomb placed inside the wall, and then covered over by the white paper that was covering the other posters around the building. Our experts informed me that the improvised pipe bomb was of a remarkably low quality, and had been set off by a timed detonator. In fact, the team estimated that even if the room had been filled to capacity, there would have been very few or perhaps even no causalities, even minor injuries. Most of the damage was to the brick and the water pipes nearby in the brick. The rector was asked, and communicated that he is unaware of anybody who would have a grudge or some reason to harm

47

the church. There are currently no suspects. The rector informed us that there
are dozens of individuals who have keys to the building, and records of such
people are not maintained in any sort of a registry. The building is occasionally
accessed by vagrants who use the building mostly for sleeping. With no real
reason to suspect the device was targeted to anyone at the church, we presumed
at this point that the intention was to disrupt the election, including harming
voters. We made a call at this point to the Department of Homeland Security
and also the Fairfax County election commissioner. At approximately 6:25 a.m.
multiple election inspectors and the precinct chairperson had arrived at the
building expecting to open doors for 7:00 voting. We informed them that a
thorough search of the building would need to take place before the building
was deemed safe, as per standard protocol. The County Director received our
recommendations to vacate the building for the day, and directed voters to
a nearby precinct. These conversations were in progress at approximately 6:45
a.m., in the parking lot of the church. Members of the media began to gather and
ask questions. I was standing in the vicinity of the County Elections Director,
Mr. Breyer, when he received a concerning message that instructed him to
redirect voters to the other precinct, to "stand firm" against calls to cancel
the precinct altogether. This message was followed by a series of potentially
damaging or embarrassing facts about Mr. Breyer and his loved ones. This was
followed by a message saying "Yes, you are being blackmailed. Do as I say." Mr.
Breyer reported this to me directly and immediately. Although the "damaging"
information about Mr. Breyer was not very damning, it seemed that there was
a clear attempt to blackmail Mr. Breyer, forcing his hand. Obviously this
raised immediate red flags. We sent bomb squads ASAP to the other polling
location, who directed inspectors to clear out even as voters lined up awaiting the
opening. At 6:57 Mr. Breyer received a text message saying "you have failed"
and the message was accompanied by a link to a news article with information
about the church bomb. The article asserted that Mr. Breyer had written
a strange clause into the financial arrangements for precinct elections, which
directed a large amount of money into a fund in the rare case that polling
places changed locations on voting day. Mr. Breyer reported the accompanying
document was forged. There was suggestion that this contract would give his
brother-in-law a windfall of $50,000 in consulting fees. The implication was

that Mr. Breyer intentionally devised a weak detonation for the very purpose of activating this clause. Further, the article appeared to display photos of Mr. Breyer at a casino, and suggested that Mr. Breyer was deeply in debt due to a gambling addiction. Now all of the accusations in the article have been shown to be demonstrably false. Mr. Breyer volunteered to make statements "on the record" immediately declaring that the accusations in the article were unequivocally false. Mr. Breyer produced documents which support this. We were in contact with Homeland Security throughout the morning, and kept them advised of this development. They informed us at this time that several other elections officials had received similar threats - they were warned not to cancel precinct activities. Curiously, some were told they were to cancel and move polling locations to nearby precincts. The motivation was unclear, and this was concerning. As we all know now, at approximately 7:30 a.m. the now infamous blockchain message appeared, suggesting that there would be a series of bombings throughout the country. It was now reported in the media that the church bomb had gone off prematurely, it was also believed that the message had been posted prematurely. We also received disturbing information about the timer device used in the explosive: We were able to contact the retailer, who reported that 800 of these devices had been sold in early October, which, to give comparison, about 50 of these devices are sold in a typical month, according to the retailer. We continued to investigate the bomb at the church. Thus far we have not changed our conclusions, namely, that this was a poorly devised explosive, probably not intended to do much harm. We have no leads on who may have been able to access the interior of the church to plant the device. Homeland Security took on the much larger investigation into the motivations for the bomb, including the possibility that it was intended as a hoax.

4

TESTIMONY OF THE SECOND WITNESS. Mr. Scott Greywahl, CEO, Tapboard, Inc.

CHAIR : The session will come to order. Thank you, ladies and gentleman for your attention in the earlier session. Our next witness Scott Greywahl has already been before a number of Senates committees, so I don't think he needs much of an introduction. I now recognize the ranking member.

SILVA : Thank you, Mr. Chairman, and thank you Mr. Greywahl, for appearing here. These hearings we are undertaking now are an attempt to understand the whats, whos, hows and at this point the whys behind the recent attack on our elections. Earlier we heard from Paul Preston, and we're hoping you could fill in a little bit more of a thorough picture. As we all know by now, the attacks on the election were funded using Tapcoin, which has been the world's most popular cryptocurrency, running on the Ricci platform. Tapcoin was pioneered by Tapboard a few years back and has since become one of the most commonly used currencies around the globe. Much of the misinformation was distributed rapidly on Tapboard. In short, it appears the election attack was financially facilitated largely by Tapcoin, and the misinformation was facilitated largely by Tapboard. We will talk about precautionary measures in the future, but at least for the time being, we'd like to know, from your vantage point, what happened in the recent election, especially as we prepare for a second attempt next week. So to begin, let's start with the coin, could you run through a quick history of Tapcoin?

GREYWAHL : Tapcoin itself, in the fully live decentralized version, is about 5 years old. We were running sort of a beta network that only confirmed transactions on our servers for many months prior, but we went live with a fully decentralized coin about 5 years ago. We had a previous version, in the early days of Tapboard, that wasn't designed to scale like the current coin. After studying the Ricci protocol, we teamed up with EWD to create a stablecoin on top of the Alice blockchain. Tapcoin is a stablecoin, in that it's pegged to a basket of global currencies. Alice is many iterations along and precedes Tapcoin by several years. The value of Alice coins are quite volatile, as is typical for untethered currencies. Tapcoin has proved quite stable, it runs on a hybrid stabilizing model, using fiat, treasury bond and crypto asset backing, as well as a very sophisticated seigniorage layer. The motto is "deep and wide". So far this coin has remained stable and functions well. Being fully decentralized, it has never experienced any downtime. The coin was designed to be a fully functional coin apart from Tapboard, as well as a programmable coin that has access to all of the programming functionality available with Alice.

SILVA : What sort of reserves are backing Tapcoin?

GREYWAHL : As I said, this is a hybrid model. There are actually several reserves - we have multiple non-profits in multiple jurisdictions which each maintain reserves, mostly government paper. The ratio as of today is about 6 to 1; that is, for every 6 Tapcoins there is about 1 Tapcoin worth of government paper. This ratio is a security parameter and can float around with time. The purpose of the reserves is not so much to back the coin but to generate interest and hedge against fluctuations in the forex market. Not hedge as in, minimize losses, but as in keep the algorithms backing the coin running smoothly so that the consumer doesn't absorb any ripples in the market. Again, the coin is generated by seigniorage bonds.

SILVA : And how much Tapcoin is out there?

GREYWAHL : Right now, as of around noon today, we're slightly above 15 trillion USD. Interestingly, the market capitalization of Alice is slightly above that range as well.

Silva : And who runs Tapcoin?

Greywahl : Well, you know, this is a decentralized currency so, technically no one can say that they run it. Tapboard uses Tapcoin as the native currency for most of our applications, including TapTrade, TapTurk, TapInstant, and so forth, but we don't actually run the underlying protocol. It's a protocol. Alice is a blockchain with an associated currency. The underlying protocol for Alice is the Ricci protocol, which is maintained by EWD in Singapore. They also provide the support for Tapcoin. Of course, they don't really, run Tapcoin, per se, so much as write the code that each network update operates from. The actual transactions are confirmed by thousands of stakeholders, most of whom are unknown, hailing from around the globe. It so happens that as we speak, Tapboard is actively exploring a potentially long and involved process to phase Tapcoin out, in favor of what we feel is a better stablecoin, called Taplite. This will run on our own in house BFT protocol, and we think this won't have some of the vulnerabilities that Tapcoin did - and will be an order of magnitude faster. I'm becoming convinced that there are many advantages of centralization.

Silva : Please describe the role of EWD in a little bit more detail.

Greywahl : EWD has been developing the Ricci protocol for about 15 years now. They designed a really solid protocol from scratch, after writing a number of sophisticated and peer-reviewed mathematical papers. I think a little bit too sophisticated, if you were to ask me. The software was designed by the same team that now maintains it. There are several cryptocurrencies that are based on the same protocols, but Tapcoin is by far the most widely adopted. Both Alice and Tapcoin come with a so-called "treasury fund" which is funded within the protocol. This fund pays EWD for maintaining the codebase. At the start of every epoch a transaction happens which funds the treasury in order to keep the maintenance team at EWD paid. For Tapcoin maintenance, the treasury is paid via seignorage bonds derived from the stablecoin. Tapboard began collaborating with EWD several years ago - our goal was to develop a stablecoin that worked well with our partially decentralized messaging and social networking app, and also that would form a basis for our full service exchange: stock, bonds, options, and crypto-assets - TapTrade. Our belief was that by leveraging the global network of the messaging app as well as our engagement in global financial markets and global commerce, we could create a stablecoin living up to the hype. That collaboration was very successful, as you can see - much of the world's business now happens with Tapcoin. Once the protocol was developed and the coin went live, about 5 to 6 years ago, we work less collaboratively with EWD. My job is to run the social network, trading and marketplace applications. EWD maintains the coin.

SILVA : How would you describe your relationship with EWD and Mr. Preston?

GREYWAHL : At the moment, not so good. When I first met Mr. Preston years ago, I admit to being somewhat mesmerized by his fascinating mathematics. He impressed me at the time as some sort of singular genius. His genius is that he is able to bring people together, I do admit that. His team has done the seminal research leading to a feasible stablecoin and this is good. But Paul himself has an ego which I find difficult to work with. Tapcoin is the greatest blockchain product ever invented, at this time, but has some vulnerabilities, and we must not be blind towards those, considering the magnitude and scope of this currency. Over the last couple years, since Alice went to the proverbial moon as Tapcoin use grew exponentially, I've learned a little bit more about how EWD and Paul operate. So we've been looking to decouple from EWD.

SILVA : Do you care to the describe the nature of your conflict?

GREYWAHL : There could be pending litigation. I will omit the aspects not germane to the conversation at hand. Suffice to say I think EWD is, well, lacks a basic transparency that could lead one to believe there are some underhanded dealings. The details would bore you nearly to death.

SILVA : Perhaps you could tell us about your frustrations, that you've mentioned in other forums, with the so-called treasury?

GREYWAHL : Sure. I'd like to talk about that because I think the discussion would give you a flavor of how lack of transparency can be frustrating.

Also, I think this story is a good example of the kind of downside that goes along with a completely decentralized currency. By the way, I very much appreciate the opportunity to speak to you about these issues. It's very important that congress takes a proactive role in understanding cryptocurrency so that the regulations are meaningful and not force-fed by financial industry lobbyists.

SILVA : Please.

GREYWAHL : Alice is a delegated proof-of-stake blockchain. Tapcoin is a stablecoin issued on top of Alice and administered by a network of contracts and a central bank that resides on the Alice blockchain. The software for Alice itself is incredibly complicated, hundreds of thousands of lines of code. This codebase is regularly updated by EWD in order to add more features and more security patches, and this requires a pretty big team. Fair enough. But the way this team is funded is via what's called a treasury - like I said - periodically, some amount of payment is minted and sent to the treasury account, which is currently held by EWD. The purpose of this arrangement is such that the currency is always maintained by a fully-salaried team of professionals and experts. Dedicating funds directly to this team ensures, at least in theory, that there will always be heavy competition for this role. Now I should go back a bit, there are two treasuries that concern Tapcoin - one is a treasury funding the development and maintenance of Alice and there is another treasury funding the maintenance of Tapcoin. At the moment, both funds are being given to teams at EWD. Now in theory, in theory, the protocol was designed so that all the stakeholders could have a discussion, if they so wish, and vote and choose a different company to whom to pay out the maintenance funds, but practically, this is never going to happen: All of the experts in the core software are employed by EWD. This means they get to essentially charge whatever they want - there's not any real competition. They claim there's competition, because in theory, again, in theory, anyone can put a bid to run the treasury and the stakeholders could vote. Practically, this would never happen. It's akin to the claim of democracy in a one-party nation state. It's not really democracy. If you are a world-class DeFi developer and want to develop on Ricci, you work for EWD. They recruit all of the top graduates from Princeton, Stanford, etc. They offer these kids $20 million out of college, to sign an NDA and work for them. So there is an undeniable hegemony. While this monopoly holds true for the treasury maintaining Alice, it's even more true for the treasury dedicated to the maintenance of Tapcoin, which again is, in principle, an independent entity, but in practice it's not. It's the 7th floor of the EWD building while the 8th floor is Alice. Literally. The governance is slightly different, importantly there is a difference in how they are funded. The Alice treasury is funded directly in Alice, while due to the structure of Tapcoin it is impossible, for very good reasons technically, to mint Tapcoins out of thin air - instead the treasury is paid in terms of seignorage bonds. These bonds have immediate market value and are essentially as good as cash. So what is the problem? Well, due to the de facto monopoly I am describing the Alice coin is being devalued, as there are payments of about $200 Billion a year for a team of several hundred software developers. Most Alice holders don't notice this because demand for the coin overall is increasing. The devaluation of Alice might not seem so bad for Tapcoin, because Tapcoin is stable, but the algorithms that maintain the stability become more vulnerable if the price of Alice were to crash. Also, by classical legal contract we (Tapboard) are required to keep a considerable stake in Alice, and Alice is supported on Tapboard as one of the currencies. Many of our users use Alice, and they like this. So devaluing Alice is bad for business. But this isn't the main concern. The most distressing part for the stability of Tapcoin is the issuance of these bonds. These create the potential to flood the bond market for this type of security, meaning the stablecoin is much less stable in the case of a blackswan event. The bond market was supposed to remain liquid but rather thin - mechanisms in place to buy and sell bonds by the central bank contract require that there is elasticity in the price. In fact the parameters designed years ago by the cryptoeconomic engineers are designed specifically to tweak the liquidity and elasticity of this secondary bond market. However, in the issuance of these bonds, the recommended parameters have been completely disregarded. The added danger is small - it's a small change of a very small probability, but even a slight change of error is unacceptable when stakes are this high. The stablecoin is based on some very solid algorithms, and a catastrophic loss of value is something near a seven sigma event. This is how it was presented to us years ago. But this required that a number of parameters stayed with certain ranges. Unfortunately, these dynamic parameters have slowly been floating well outside the safe range, and because of the nature of the proposal process, there is little that stakeholders can do about this. Again, this is due to the complete monopoly that EWD has over the governance of the blockchain.

SILVA : Slow down for a minute. I'm sorry. These parameters, it seems you are telling me the network requires certain parameters to run, and these are essential to security.

GREYWAHL : Yes, indeed.

SILVA : So who determines these parameters?

GREYWAHL : OK. Well, these are proposed - it's slightly complicated, but essentially these are proposed and accepted by a vote. Often the treasury proposals will include the parameters, but there are built-in ways to tweak them if necessary.

SILVA : A vote by who?

GREYWAHL : Stakeholders of Alice. If you own Alice, you get to vote. The rules are a bit messy. But it's all "democratic." These are security parameters, so the theory has always been that those who hold the largest quantities of Alice should have the largest vested interested in preserving the security. There is a notion of "wisdom of the crowd" baked in the design of the security consensus.

SILVA : That certainly makes sense. Please continue.

GREYWAHL : It does make sense until you understand the exploits, but I'll come back to that I'm sure. As I was describing, if the Alice currency is ever being devalued too quickly, bad parameter values raise the probability of a catastrophic crash quite considerably - still rare and unlikely in the foreseeable future, but with all of the businesses currently operating on Tapcoin, we need to keep this probability as close to absolute zero as possible. One percent is way too high. A stablecoin losing its value would be an unheard of economic catastrophe. Call me a "parameter-scold" all you want, but I think I'm in good company. There is considerable debate in the community about where the parameters should lie, and there is, quite unfortunately, a significant portion of the community that believes these discussions of parameters are merely a joke. These parameter-scoffs tend to be these self-described "autodidacts" who finished half a year in community college and made a couple lucky trades and think they know something about cryptocurrency. They pose a danger. To be fair, so far, the effect hasn't been so pronounced, because I think a lot of enthusiasm and demand has stepped up to meet this excess money that is being printed, but the longer this goes, I mean, you can't just keep printing $200 Billion a year and not end up with a glut and a crash. Many businesses operate primarily on Tapboard, and pay their employees and bills in Tapcoin. It would be a consummate disaster if the currency were to falter.

SILVA : So is Tapcoin bound by any sort of contractual relations with EWD?

GREYWAHL : There was an agreement, but the continued development is not bound by contract. We are free to go where we want. This is both, I guess you would say, a bug and a feature. We developed Tapcoin on Alice working closely with EWD because we both had common interests. This was wildly successful for us, and them, a few years back, but now we're tied into the Tapcoin ecosystem until we can onboard our other currency - but this takes some time and effort. Our users use Tapcoin and are largely happy with it.

SILVA : So the treasury is a certain - account? - which historically has belonged to EWD - that is given newly created funds, and the members of the network are able to vote on the recipient of the treasury funds?

GREYWAHL : Yes. They get to vote on treasury proposals, which are essentially an account together with a price. Anyone can bid, but EWD is the only account that ever is approved. Sometimes they offer multiple proposals.

There's also a mechanism so that the treasury defaults to the last accepted situation in the case no new bid is approved. It turns out that the funding, which ends up being this ridiculous amount, always ends up being funded. $200 Billion a year for about 150 developers. They charge essentially $1 billion per year per developer. I now for a fact the developers only receive a fraction of that. This is strange, my suspicion (if I'm allowed to offer my suspicion in this setting) is that EWD is being coerced somehow, and perhaps redistributing these funds elsewhere.

SILVA : So you believe that $200 billion per year are being minted and passed to someone using some sort of coercion? Do you have evidence of this?

GREYWAHL : No direct evidence, only inference from observations. My engineers have looked at some of the contracts and flagged them as suspicious, but often it's hard to tell what exactly they do. Often these appear on the dark side chains, the so-called darkMAs, so you can't read what the contract does, but you can guess by a couple of other features of the contract what it might be used for. But this is really really rough.

SILVA : And what are these observations?

GREYWAHL : Right. There is no good reason that the treasury and stakeholders would keep approving this sort of inflationary money printing. Unlike Bitcoin, where the money supply is fixed, the money supply for Alice is more fluid and is constantly recalibrated. But everyone almost everywhere agrees that it's best to keep inflation to a minimum. This is a community value. Most of the developers, stakeholders and decision makers share the same values. No one wants to see their coin devalued. In fact there was a hard limit set years ago, that supposedly you could not go above - this was overridden many times, with community approval. So my guess is that somehow, the devaluation that the stakeholders are agreeing to must be favorable when compared to some other option. I don't know what the other option is, but I am guessing that this other option is being presented to the treasury and is very unpleasant. That's why I suspect coercion: There is something bad, much worse than inflation, that the decisionmakers are protecting against. There's many ways this could appear, if you have some imagination, but for example, it could be a major stakeholder, threatening to dump their coins all at once, and sending the whole thing crashing down. Or there might be some other action they can take as a major stakeholder to devalue the coin, or worse, threaten the stablecoin.

SILVA : You are suggesting that one party is threatening to sell all of their Alice coins at one time, and using this as leverage?

GREYWAHL : Maybe, this is one possibility for a leveraged play.

SILVA : And these coins would go directly to the party making these threats?

GREYWAHL : Presumably, yes. We can't do a direct audit of EWD, and it's hard for any authority to ever do because they exist inside an onion of international LLCs, but it would be completely reasonable that EWD is paying a large, you know, "security consultation" fee to some entity. I should stress I'm just speculating. This is pure speculation.

SILVA : Wow, this sounds like quite a racket. But what strikes me as a bit odd here, is, the question of why one would believe they would follow through? Wouldn't this ending up hurting themselves more than the parties they are threatening?

GREYWAHL : It's not clear who would hurt the most, but right, they would be shooting themselves in the foot so to speak - at least in the situation where a major stakeholder is threatening damage to the ecosystem.

SILVA : So why does the treasury respond to these threats?

GREYWAHL : Because they would be credible. What happens quite often now is that threats will be made that can be enforced by smart contract. You simply state your condition that needs to be met, hash this into a smart contract, and then let the other parties know. The smart contract will take care of the rest in the unfortunate situation where your conditions aren't met. This way you can take the option out of your own hands and your threat becomes credible. For example, someone could write a smart contract that would sell $1 trillion worth of coins for 1/10 of market price. The contract becomes activated if, say, a certain account hasn't received new coins by say next Thursday. So if the account isn't credited the coins by Thursday, everybody knows this contract is going to dump the coins and send the market spiraling. Nobody wants this so, you know, you give the extortionist the coins.

SILVA : These threats are built into smart contracts?

GREYWAHL : Yes, and this is becoming hard to combat and quite frequent. It's quite a plague. It's child's play for a number of leeching organizations throughout the world. I'm guessing that's what going on here. It's completely possible that whoever is making these threats has built up a huge stake, enough to play this game for a while into the future. Eventually it breaks and the whole system comes crashing down, but you can probably get away with this for awhile. But the bad situation is bad for everybody. Very bad.

SILVA : How long have you been on the outs with EWD?

GREYWAHL : A few years. When they took Bitcoin head-on, I was completely blindsided. I would have liked a heads-up. We had been working very closely in tandem to implement Tapcoin as a currency for Tapboard and had just launched this quite successfully. I heard from a lot of friends and business partners around the world hurt by the attack on Bitcoin and most of these people haven't forgiven me. Even though I had nothing to do with this. The timing was very suspicious, you know, this new currency is launched at the same time a coordinated attack on Bitcoin is perpetrated. This attack was Da, Paul and who knows who else. They didn't clue me in despite the fact that the whole operation heavily involved the currency we had developed together. They told me "Good news, your net worth just went up $500 Billion". We've had a very rocky relationship since then. I think Bitcoin was wasteful, but I don't know if I would've supported this. Bitcoin was going to die on it's own good time.

SILVA : I'd like to ask you directly: Has Tapboard entertained any hopes that future elections will be run on Tapboard, or on a blockchain?

GREYWAHL : I've heard the accusations you're suggesting and have to say that frankly this makes no sense. Even if we are working on elections technology, and of course we've thought of this, we would want this to be secure and simple, why would we throw our own platform into chaos and destroy any credibility? This would be counterproductive. We obviously have some work to do before this becomes a reality. But this is, I think, a very wide goal of many in the blockchain space. I can guarantee you everyone in the space has entertained the idea of running elections on a blockchain. It absolutely has to be permissioned - I wouldn't dream of putting an election on a decentralized blockchain. I'm sorry that's just begging for trouble.

SILVA : Thank You. You've indicated that you would like to transition to a different blockchain? Is this based on extortion? other reasons?

GREYWAHL : As I've said, my assessment is that EWD is being extorted themselves. There's a bunch of funny contracts that are tied to the treasury account, these are a bit difficult to unravel, but my engineers have told me they believe these are maybe ransomware embedded in the blockchain - so EWD's hands are tied. Not my problem, though, not my customers' problem. Philosophically, Paul and the team in general at EWD are very much opposed to permissioned blockchains - they are contractarianist ideologues, and have always been. They believe permissioned blockchains are antithetical to the very ethos of blockchain. When Tapcoin was created, we created a board of economists, mathematicians, businessmen, and they meet regularly to monitor the chain and make recommendations. This is purely an advisory board, they have no power. In the early days, they would make recommendations in regards to small tweaks of the money supply, staking pledge parameters, in fact there are 29 parameters that go into Tapcoin at the moment. Back then, the board would make recommendations that would typically be approved by the stakeholder elections, and the treasury in charge of creating new proposals and amendments would build the recommendations into proposals. But recently, we've seen a bit of a divergence. A significant portion of the community fails to understand why the parameter recommendations are what they are, and as a result you get coalitions that oppose these parameters. You often end up with parameters that are not 100% secure, in my opinion. The chance of anything going wrong this year, or next year, is quite small, so only the experts sit around and fret about these things. But the risk is not optimal and I am quite nervous that if the parameters continue to float away from safe regions we may end up with a very insecure blockchain. So for the benefit and security of our users on Tapboard, we are moving to a permissioned blockchain. I'm not sure that it is possible to avoid the sort of attacks that can plague a fully decentralized chain. This isn't popular with the diehards, but at this point I don't think we have any other option. In the end, people just like the convenience of these stablecoin transactions, and don't really care about the politics of decentralization. Probably 99% of Tapboard's users are not buying drugs or anything illegal, and aren't trying to get away with tax evasion. So permissioned is fine for most people. They like the feel and user experience, not that anti-government whacko conspiracy whacko nonsense that motivated the initial fervor behind blockchain.

Of course, I should point out that this is a delicate thing. We plan to phase it out somewhat gradually, as we're slightly worried about what sort of damage would happen to Alice if the bottom were to drop out. Because Tapcoin is a stablecoin, we can enact a scheduled transition to make sure nothing crashes. Even better, because we plan to keep the issuance and swapping control centralized, we have much more flexibility. Long term, this should mean some loss of value to Alice. Many of our shareholders and employees have been paid in Tapcoin and some have opted to take payment in Alice, so we really don't want to spook the market. There's a potential for a reverse 'suckening' if we are not too careful.

SILVA : Reverse suckening?

GREYWAHL : Right. About 4 years ago when Tapcoin was scaling rapidly, there was a lot of fluctuation in demand for various currencies and other instruments such as treasuries. All of a sudden there was massive demand for these sort of paper reserves and there was quite a bit that was sucked away from typical markets. Obviously it wasn't catastrophic, most people were somewhat protected from this but a couple of hedge funds tried to fight it and went belly-up. It's very hard to predict exactly how these things will play out, so you have to be careful. I don't want to give a timetable yet. But we will take a broad and unselfish view. But I should say, in the initial testing phases of Taplite, which we can do on our own because it's centralized and the tests reflect how it will actually perform, let me tell you, Taplite is going to melt faces. This will be the fastest, microsecond financial technology ever. We have 100's of satellites positioned around the world that are relaying transactions. So the speed of light is literally the limitation. Once you remove the decentralization, you will see faces melt. The capabilities -

SILVA : I'm sorry, this sounds promising but I want to go back to this extortion, you claim this is probably a major stakeholder, can you guess who this might be?

GREYWAHL : Actually, I gave you sort of a standard rather simple example which doesn't require a lot of explanation. This could be the case, it could be this easy. I'm guessing that in reality we're dealing with a slightly less obvious attack. There are actually much more subtle attacks of a similar nature, which don't require the same amount of risk. There's another attack - and I think this might be more likely. To begin, I should say that when all these academics wrote these game theory papers a decade ago, they made a number of assumptions, for example, that it was irrational for an attacker to operate for an extended period of time at a loss, and also that it would not be easy to borrow a significant portion of the coin, and most dangerously, the assumption was that self-governance would somehow be rational - you know, the wisdoms of crowds would average out to reasonable governance arrangements. It makes sense for each individual to behave rationally, locally in time. This makes sense locally in time, for an individual - if I'm just anybody, trying to stake a few coins and earn a little bit on top of my holdings, I'm not going to doing anything untoward that will mess up the system. But if I'm really intent on attacking the system, and I can stomach operating at a loss, I may be able do a few things to frustrate or grief the system, especially if I can borrow a little bit of coin.

Just to go back, if you recall: Proof of Stake is a system in which your reward for participating in confirming the next block is proportional to the amount of the coin you have. The problem with the most naive implementation of this system is that in order for the average person to take advantage of this, they have to have their computer online and running a node, at all times, so that they can occasionally get a small reward. Most people don't run nodes, it's just not rational and it's wasteful. So if all the small scale users are passing on their opportunity, then the staking and validating - that is - performing some basic bookkeeping in exchange for the small rewards that go to those selected randomly to create the next block - if most users are passing on this, then it's possible that either the staking is not getting done, in which case transactions aren't getting processed, or; you get a small group of heavy players who are doing everything. The descent into oligarchy is rapid.

This latter situation is the sort of oligarchy we strive to avoid - it's a security hazard as well - if only a few people are in charge of the mining, and they don't have a lot to lose, they can nuke the whole system with the right motivation. So the solution is what they call Delegated Proof of Stake. Delegated Proof of Stake means that you can assign your fraction to someone else who is going to do the bookkeeping - you then split the reward. Usually the way this works out is that if your expectation for staking over a week or so is $20, instead of having a computer running a full node the whole time, you can delegate your portion to a stake pool - and they will charge you a small fee, say 10%. So each week you get $18. You get to choose which pool you join - that way it's competitive, if someone is only charging 5% - you go with them and make an extra dollar each week. This is what most everyday users do - they just have a staking pool.

Now there are many ways to do Delegated Proof of Stake. The BFC project learned the hard way a few years back that all methods are not equal. BFC designed a protocol where you do some sort of voting and election and a finite number, I think it was 31, pool operators are chosen to run the chain. But this wasn't very well thought out, and some researchers pointed out that you could essentially gain control of 16 of the nodes with 3.1% of the outstanding BFC. Very few people listened to the researchers. But at some point, when the marketcap was something near $80 Billion, a group, or an individual, nobody knows, but we think this is how GP came about, this group wanted to make some money with a dramatic short. So they went out and were able to borrow about $5 Billion worth of BFC. (How this happened is an international regulatory black-eye). They then were able to manage to sell it with a future delivery date about three weeks in the future. Now because they actually held this much coin in the meantime, they were able to gain control of 23 of the nodes. They trashed the network for about 9 days and the price dropped by 85%, at which point they bought enough to cover the short. They made off with several billion dollars, and the network never recovered. This was a major boon for Alice, as enterprise applications flocked away from BFC and towards Alice.

Fortunately, the cryptonomic engineers at EWD are significantly more sophisticated, they use non-myopic game theory and test it using dynamic simulations, so it's going to be several orders of magnitude more robust. They had a different solution: Instead of having a finite number of delegates, allow anyone who would like to run a staking pool, and users can choose where to stake. Now of course you're probably thinking - won't this just lead to a situation in which there's like one or two big staking pools? Yes, well, the engineers thought of this and came up with something to thwart this - the maximum amount that any individual pool can receive as rewards is a small number, say 1% of the total. So if 2% of the all the holdings are staked with one pool, these accounts are only going to have half of what they otherwise would be earning if they staked in a pool that wasn't larger than 1%. This keeps the size of the pool small - from a staker's perspective, you don't want to join a pool that's bigger than 1%. There were usually a little more than 100 pools - they tried to operate at full capacity and with low fees. Now you may ask, what about a Sybil attack? Nothing stops a group or individual from opening dozens of staking pools, right? The engineers created a staking multiple parameter so that the pool leader is required to have a minimum stake and the reward of the stake pool depends on how much is pledged by the pool operators. Now there's a bit of a balance and nuance in this parameter. If you make this parameter too high, you end up in a situation where only a few of the richer stakeholders can actually stake. This is what happened for a while, and while no one had too large of a share, it was easy for the wealthy stakeholder to collude to raise prices. That $20 you thought you could earn was now $3, which is better than nothing, but not enough to make you figure out how to run a full node. So there was demand to drop this parameter down a bit so that there was more competition. The competition was real, and what happened is that different pool leaders decided they were OK to operate at a slight loss, you can charge negligible or 0% fees. Most users will be attracted to a few extra dollars a month, so they will opt for one of your pools. This gives you market share. You can hike the prices and most users won't go through the hassle of changing stake pools over $3/month. We think this has started to happen - in fact the staking pools started offering negative fees - paying a 10% extra reward for switching your stake, for a short period of time. Now this isn't so bizarre - credit cards and banks and phone companies are always throwing cash rewards at customers trying to get them to switch. But the odd thing is that the "short term" bonus is like, 18 months into the future - which means these pools will be losing quite a bit of rewards for a while, maybe thousands of dollars a day. I can only conclude they are playing some other long game. It's concerning because it's not so obvious what the game is. The other aspect of this that is concerning to me is the way the parameters have floated out of safe regions.

As you can imagine, I'm oversimplifying slightly. There's actually about 20 parameters that go into the Alice protocol (there's 9 extra for Tapcoin). Many of these are decided by decentralized governance. Recently the recommendations of the board have been disregarded. The problem is that you have hundreds of stake pool operators, and the purpose of these stake pools is to make money. Each parameter change effects each stakeholder in some way, depending on their stake share, their costs, and their share of the market for stakers. It's very nonlinear, depending on the Gini distribution of stake, among other things. So each of these pool operators lobby the decentralized stakeholders on the virtues of different parameter values. Oftentimes, a small change in the parameters can only slightly weaken the security of the chain, but result in heavy advantage for one pool operator or another, or at least one strata of pool operators. There's a lot of money involved. This is how and why the parameters float around. Most pool operators are less worried about the long-term stability of the system and more worried about the current epoch. Alice itself is almost a decade old, and hasn't had any major attacks. Probably, it's too big to attack. That's the conventional wisdom, at least. But nonetheless, it makes me quite nervous that parameter values are regularly being flown in the face of expert recommendations. There hasn't been an obvious attack on the network, yet. But I'm seeing pools operating at a loss, while the treasury is paid quite heavily.

SILVA : So you believe that some anonymous parties are operating in a way that ostensibly is unprofitable in order to control the chain?

GREYWAHL : You've followed the lecture quite well, professor. That's exactly what we're guessing. And what I think is going on is that they are siphoning off treasury funds, using the leverage of completely disrupting the blockchain, they are using this as leverage against EWD, essentially increasing the cost of operations. Now this is not simply a wild conjecture, this sort of malicious abuse has been creeping through the crypto ecosystem in a practice that goes by the term leverballing.

SILVA : Please explain leverballing.

GREYWAHL : Leverballing is the following. I guess in a nutshell, it's just your classic extortion, but with digital currency, and digital threats. It proceeds as follows, I obtain some means to destroy something of value, something you derive value from, and I threaten you and tell you that I have the power to do it. Usually, because of all the mechanisms set up in the designs of consensus protocols, this will be a very expensive threat for me to follow through with. That's the basis for the security of the digital coins in general: You really have to spend a lot of money just to mess with the consensus a little bit. Thus no one would ever be motivated to make the effort to mess with anything. This is why and how Bitcoin held up so well for so many years. No one is willing to outlay the expense to disrupt it.

It's very expensive and the payoff is hard to engineer. But, but the real question, coming from an economist's point of view, if you can think like John Nash for a minute - the question is the following: Is the cost to me of destroying X more or less than the cost to you if this X is destroyed? If so, it creates sort of an arbitrage opportunity, if you do it carefully and have the means to pull it off. Essentially, suppose I can spend $1 million in order to cost you $2 million. Obviously I don't want to do this, unless I just have some spite for you or something, but otherwise, you know, that's $1 million I could do something else with. However, if you stand to lose $2 million, this becomes a leverballing opportunity. All I have to do is show to you that I'm serious about following through on the threat. Then, you'll pay me not to do it, provided that you believe I'm willing to follow through with my threat. This is something Professor Nash studied - and the canonical agreement is called the Nash Bargaining Solution. Nash viewed the outcome that I spend the money to grief you, that is, I lose $1 million and you lose $2 million as the "base point" - what economists call the "disagreement point". If you start with that assumption instead, then suddenly it changes your mentality. You see me not pulling the trigger as an opportunity to gain $2 million, so you're willing to pay me so that I can gain and you can gain. In fact Nash conjectured a unique solution, the solution being that we split the difference and you pay me $500,000 not to cost you $2 million. The problem with Nash's original viewpoint was that this was highly mathematical and "translationally invariant" and didn't really get down to the nuts and bolts of practical game theory: In the real world the more important question is often: "who's move is it?" and "who benefits from the current position?" These questions matter in practice. There was no way to actually move the situation away from where neither of us are losing money to where both of us are losing money, without, of course, some sort of guarantee of both of us losing if we can't come to an agreement. The problem of tactical negotiations arriving at the Nash Bargaining Solution was an open problem in economics for a while. Now an economist named Rubinstein (perhaps you know him - I think he's still at NYU) suggested that if we are allowed to use some probability, then suddenly the Nash Bargaining Solution becomes feasible. To go back to my example: if there is a small, say 1% chance, every day, that I'm going to spend $1 million to cost you $2 million dollars unless we both agree on something- and this 1% event is out of my control - then the base point becomes this disagreement point and now we are not so much trying to avoid losing money, but trying to decide how to split the proceeds each of us will get from not losing the money. It's a different way of thinking. If you offer two people $100 to split, provided they can agree on how to split it, they will usually split the difference and agree. So now the arrangement is in my favor - I can propose some reasonable price to permanently destroy this mechanism, and you will accept the offer and we will both go our merry ways. When Rubinstein proposed this it was sort of just an academic economic argument, with some nice mathematics. It wasn't until we had fully operating smart contracts that it became possible to fully realize this. It required a clever bit of engineering, but by now it is technically script-kiddie's play to write a smart contract that runs on a blockchain that can perform some action with a probability. The contract can either be shutdown by it's owner, or, the contract is shutdown by observing some condition (like a payment to a certain address) but each day, or epoch or whatever, the contract does some probabilistic computation and decides whether to trigger some event or not. I can write a contract that will release $1 million of my own money in a maliciously designed way that will cost you $2 million of grief, and have this action set to happen with probability 1% each week unless you pay me. There's a number of ways to do this, especially with Bounties. But anyways, suppose I've set this contract to trigger with 1% probability, and suppose I tell you this, and then I let this contract run and I don't kill the contract. After a week of seeing the contract run, you have to assume I'm going to keep letting the contract run until we both get screwed, but you worse than I, so you offer me $500,000. I take it and terminate the contract. If you're stubborn or spiteful I can let the contract run for a while - there's still some game of chicken involved here, there's always a game of chicken, but I can run it for 10 weeks at an expected lost of $100,000 - your expected loss is $200,000. Eventually you should give in and pay.

SILVA : I believe I'm with you so far, this brings me to back - I spent a semester in graduate school studying Thomas Schelling, so it's interesting to see this played out. Doesn't this just amount to blackmail or extortion?

GREYWAHL : Well of course. But this is blockchain. Code is law. There are no governing authorities that are going to step in and say "sorry that's unethical." In fact, much of what is done is technically legal, some isn't. While there have been examples of literally illegal blackmail, there have been plenty examples of more leveraged negotiation that is more on the legal side of things, using smart contracts.

SILVA : Legal blackmail?

GREYWAHL : Well, legally, if you retain some right to publish information, you can also use this as a leveraging tactic. I'm not a lawyer, but there's a legal notion of "nexus". Like if the information you threaten to publish has a direct connection to the topic of your negotiation, you can use this as leverage.

In fact, I helped my cousin in New Jersey use this tactic. Years ago, he had hired a contractor to do a small-scale remodel of his home. It's going OK, but one of the subs is just doing a horrible job, like damaging the home. I won't get into the details, but this sub is a total disaster. And the contractor is completely unapologetic about it. So when it's finished, my cousin blasts out this angry 1-star review, complaining about how unprofessional these guys are, blah blah blah. He gets served a $2 million lawsuit for defamation. My cousin goes to a lawyer and says, how can they do this? and the lawyer tells him, well it's New Jersey, there's no anti-SLAPP statutes here, so let's find out what they want. So they go back and forth, exchanging Christmas lists, and so forth, and after a couple of months my cousin gets a bill for $25,000 in legal fees, and also his lawyer saying, hey good news, they're willing to drop the lawsuit if you pay them $50,000 and sign an NDA. My cousin is furious and starts to do some research. The sub they've hired isn't even licensed. They've been using this sub for many of their projects and know very well he's not licensed. They've been putting fake license numbers on the invoices. It turns out a number of their subs aren't licensed. And this was supposedly a somewhat respectable design-build firm that did a lot of business. So my cousin collects this information, brings it to the lawyer, and says, bam, look at this, and the lawyer is like, what are you going to do? Go and piss them off? Don't kick the hornets' nest, just sign the damn NDA and move on with your life. My cousin is confident he has the high ground here, but the lawyer insists to him that this will just make them angry - they will spend the next 3 years trying to clear their name while destroying his. They won't win but it will cost $500,000 of legal fees and three years of stress. The lawyer, who's a partner at a big firm tells my cousin, hey, I know this from experience, don't make this worse for you and your family, sign the offer before it goes away.

When my cousin explains this to me I'm all wound up. This is before TapTurk was a thing and there was this very preliminary version of Bounties that was functional, and we came up with a plan. We collected all his research into a zipped file, hashed it, and published the hash on the blockchain. Then we sent the unhashed file to a PR firm in Philadelphia which was blockchain literate. We then set up a probabilistic bounty contract which did a couple of things. First, the contract was to run until deactivated by my cousin. As long as the contract was running, there was a 1% chance per day that the bounty would be activated. Now this was a special bounty, one that could only be redeemed by the PR firm, and it would be paid only in the case that the unhashed file was posted, and downloaded by 10,000 unique users. So it was the PR firm's job to point enough people towards this file so that they would download the docs. So my cousin takes this contract, explains how it works to the lawyer, who was clueless about this kind of thing. Then he takes it directly to the adversary and they're, like, whatever, I guess we'll take our chances. Three weeks later, the contract is activated. My cousin had also bought insurance on the contract - so it cost him money a little bit everyday to keep the contract running, but when it activated, the PR firm is now motivated by a healthy payout. So they immediately flood the web with not just digital advertising with links to download my cousin's research, but with well-placed organic looking news stories. They collect the bounty within a couple days. It turns out, surprise, surprise, there were a number of other people who had been sued or threatened with lawsuits, and this contractor had a host of legal shortcomings. They went bankrupt within a year, and lawyers were even able to pierce the veil and go after the CEOs $8 million home. It was extremely satisfying. So while the threat itself didn't work to dissuade this particular firm from pursuing the defamation claim, it did create enough of a stir that this same exact form of threat was used to quell defamation lawsuits in the future. I know of a number of other cases where the contract was created and the other party caved because they didn't want to expose themselves like the contractor had.

Now my point was that this is completely legal, because publicly posting evidence that backs up your defense of a defamation claim is fair game for negotiations.

SILVA : This use case makes sense, but I guess I need to ask another question. Back to the less ethical blockchain extortion: What stops you from just repeating this whole game? Don't we just go back to square one? I mean the problem with blackmail is that once you pay someone once, you're still back at square one, they can just threaten you again, right?

GREYWAHL : Yes, what you say is correct. But in the case where a certain player has leverage over a blockchain and is making these threats, you probably wouldn't get away with the exploit I described more than once, if that's the agreement. You can do it continuously over time, provided the arrangement seems sustainable. There's game theory and there's common sense regarding human behavior and human psychology, common in multiple senses, I suppose. If I tried to play this game more than once, obviously you ignore me the second time - once it's clear that you're ignoring me, I still have the ability to pull back. This is how humans expect each other to behave. That's the fun, perhaps I shouldn't say 'fun', but that's the perplexing thing about practical game theory - a lot is based on how we expect people to behave and work with this. Blackmail is quite ancient. The assumption that the blackmailer will not double dip from the well is sort of a Schelling Point - if blackmailers started double dipping as a general practice, they would go out of business, because nobody would trust them. I know this is not a very deep academic answer - but sometimes the answer is found in just folk understanding of human psychology.

SILVA : So your assessment is that someone was using this technique to extort EWD?

GREYWAHL : Exactly. If I have control of your blockchain, I can mess with it in a number of ways, I can disrupt it for quite an extended period of time, which will destroy confidence in the currency, make people unhappy, you lose market value. So all I really need is a way to make a threat in a way such that you will take it seriously. This can be done using other blockchains - so many blockchains are fully programmable and have state channels and oracles that allow information to input be from other places. For example, I can extort you via an Ethereum contract - this is a simple enforcement mechanism: Suppose that I have the power to disrupt the Tapcoin blockchain for an epoch. I claim that I'm going to do this. I can simply create an Ethereum contract that monitors the Tapcoin blockchain for the given epoch. If the disruptive event gets triggered, then the Ethereum contract checks the Tapcoin blockchain and determines if it has been disrupted. If not, it burns $1 million in Ethereum that I've put in escrow - and I have no control over this. Thus I force my hand. In the game of chicken, this is how I can remove the steering wheel from my vehicle.

SILVA : Ethereum and Tapcoin are different chains though right?

GREYWAHL : Yes, of course, but by now, there's a lot of interoperability, where the chains can essentially talk to each other. This is fairly straightforward stuff these days. There are contracts that basically read data from one chain to another.

SILVA : Are you aware of such a contract on Ethereum?

GREYWAHL : Not precisely, but it's really a chore to try to reverse engineer every contract out there. There are literally millions running. Too much to really monitor. We assume such a contract exists - this would explain why the treasury keeps increasing their fees for no apparent reason and many of the stake pools are operating at a loss.

SILVA : What stops users from just going with honest stakepools?

GREYWAHL : Good question - two things, first, you have to ask which ones are honest. Just because they're operating at a profit, does this mean they're honest? Secondly, and more important, the eternal problem of prisoner's dilemma at a large scale. If everybody else is going with the dishonest stake pools, we're all fine until one day we're not fine, at which point we're all screwed. There's no advantage of going with the honest pool at any particular point in time. In the short term the honest pool just means less rewards. If everybody else is honest, you can get a little extra money and not do any damage by going with the dishonest pool. That's the nature of prisoner's dilemma. The only reason not to take the larger payout would be to believe that you are the one that would tip the balance of the entire ecosystem from honest to dishonest. It's Large Poisson Games meets Ethics. If you're anywhere near this line, you just assume it's a lost cause. But again, going back to the first issue that I mentioned - it's not really clear who the bad ones are, it's not like there's a clearinghouse out there with solid information saying that these are good and these are bad. It's not like the dishonest pools have disclaimers that say "we may use your coin to destroy the blockchain". Of course it's possible that some of the staking pools are not operating at a loss rather are only pretending to, trying to optimize the rate in order to attract more accounts.

SILVA : So this sort of leveraged ransom attack is a widespread problem in cryptocurrencies?

GREYWAHL : Yes, I believe it is. I don't work directly in cryptocurrency back-end so much, but I'm aware of this as it has been described to me by a number of people on the inside, including a number of security experts. This is something that has always been on our radar. There is, or was, I don't know, a group, that called themselves "Gros Poisson". It's a fran-cophonic word play - by the way - referring to the mathematical notion of a Poisson process, and also the nature of what's going on - big fish eats little fish. This group has been giving themselves a continuous stream of money by extorting various blockchains. They have been at this business for a number of years, so they have quite a bit of leverage. For a period of time GP was behind a lot of consolidation in the blockchain space - as they would use leverage on a larger blockchain to damage or destroy smaller blockchains. This really weeded out the blockchains with weak security. For this reason many of the real serious people in the space were OK with GP, as the net effect was to cull the herd. The whole space was lousy with poorly thought-out and scammy blockchain projects, so GP expedited some very necessary consolidation. In fact, when we suspected a chain was weak and vulnerable we used to make the joke that they were going to "join the Wainwrights", referring to an old Gary Larson cartoon. It becomes trickier against the more established and well-founded blockchain projects. My guess is that they are extorting but not destroying EWD, and at this point, not really caring about being too brazen about it. I don't know if GP is big enough at the moment to do damage, but I'm uncomfortable with the risk. I'm guessing they don't want to destroy their cash cow.

Certainly Alice is big enough to avoid leveraged borrowing attacks, but this doesn't account for every attack vector out there.

SILVA : I'm curious to hear about how this Poisson process is used in the extortion?

GREYWAHL : So when they weren't directly shorting and trashing blockchains, they would use probabilistic threats. A cryptorandom Poisson process is essential to implementing these Rubinstein contracts I was discussing earlier. You can create a contract that activates a random event essentially like a Poisson process. This just means there's a predetermined probability that the contract is going to be triggered in any given time period, and it's as continuous as possible. Often for these blockchains that process 3 blocks a minute, you might have the contract randomly triggered with probability 1 out of 100,000. At this rate it will eventually be triggered in the next month or so, but probably not in the next day or hour. So when they make a threat, they accompany the threat with a live smart contract that you have to pay to turn off. There are some security parameters designed to thwart this, but it's hard for people to take these threats seriously when most blockchain projects don't have a lot of security awareness.

Behind the scenes, the engineers still take the parameters seriously, but the stakeholders, often stakeholders who vote, are easily convinced not to worry about certain problems. So risky use of the blockchain governance seems to happen. I've been sounding the alarm for years, but people call me an alarmist and a fearmongerer, a parameter-scold. But I'm hoping that something can be done. Since I'm here, with your attention, I'd like to implore you to do something. I personally would like to see blockchains forced to be permissioned, and then the operators given guidelines. So much money laundering happens with Tapcoin that I don't feel equipped to address, partially because it's not a centralized coin, but also because the regulatory guidance isn't so obvious. The US leads the world in technology, so if you lead, other nations will follow.

SILVA : So are you saying that cryptocurrency is basically unsound? Years ago there was a bit of celebratory declaration that academics had solved the underlying problems, I think Mr. Preston refers to this as the Trilemma. Are you saying that the problems emerge when guidelines are ignored? Is this sort of an inevitable problem that governance mechanisms will always struggle to maintain good practices?

GREYWAHL : Declarations that these problems had been solved were largely coming from Paul's crowd and were a bit premature, at least in my opinion. I shouldn't say premature, rather, they were a bit narrow in scope. When you read these papers, they have a certain attack model set up and they assume that everything that could go wrong follows this given attack model. Ricci's Delegated Proof of Stake model is secure against a large array of attack vectors, but most of these are only accounting for internal motivations, not external ones. Of course, reality doesn't care about your attack model.

One would be wise to be wary of Paul and his connection to Academia. Knowing Paul, I'm sure he neglected to tell you how much he spent on arranging these supposed "collaborations" with all of these universities. Paul spent billions of dollars setting up professorships and labs and endowed chairs at institutions. The point of funding these studies was to simply publicize and legitimize certain fields of study. If a Stanford CS professor is devoting research to neuroming, or a Princeton economics professor doing research on decentralized governance, you think there must be something there, right? It worked. It worked quite well. In the case of the neuromining and Komolgorov Complexity research it quickly became sort of an accepted fact that mining rigs could be repurposed for other heavy computational disciplines. Let me be clear, this Komolgorov Complexity business is like string theory, well that's probably not fair, but KCT has been the subject of thousands of papers but thus far there isn't really any evidence that practical problems are in the regime where KCT applies. Mathematicians are on a daily basis posting papers tweaking the asymptotic tail estimates, but this is just a decay rate as you go towards infinity and it's completely unclear that we're there, technologically speaking. That's not to say 5 to 10 years out we could be there, and believe me, we have a team in Paris working on this and pushing out papers, and don't get me wrong, it's crack cocaine for the mathematically inclined brain. The researchers can't put this down, but at the moment, it's not something that gives a discernible advantage in data analysis. It's probably a decade away from being useful. So when Paul goes on touting how his team has harnessed Komolgorov Complexity for using mining rigs to do supercharged machine learning research - I would view that with quite a bit of skepticism. I would view any claims made by academics about blockchain with a great deal of skepticism, as a general rule.

SILVA : OK. If we may, let's talk about the Bounties application and the role of Tapboard. There were millions of messages, posts, memes, etc., that were shared in regards to the election. Many of these were paid for using Tapcoin. Do you know how this was accomplished?

GREYWAHL : How is sort of easy, that's what the system is set up to do. Bounties is arranged so you can get paid for doing almost anything. We don't draw a line - I suppose we do we draw a line at threats of violence and, as much as legally possible, clearly false and fabricated information. We respect freedom of speech. The mechanics are simple: Users are allowed to post what they want, and what happens with the coin is often beyond our control. Bounties is the underlying protocol for TapTurk, which many people are using these days for employment. We can't take legal responsibility for everything that is done with our service.

SILVA : But Tapcoin is the native supported currency for Tapboard, and TapTurk right?

GREYWAHL : Yes, but it's a decentralized protocol. We don't control it.

SILVA : But the API is set up, deliberately, from what I've been told, so that accounts can be paid directly by smart contracts. Is this the case?

GREYWAHL : I think you are taking two things and trying to combine them in a malicious way. The Tapboard API is very powerful, and the cryptocurrency smart contract API is very expressive and yes, you can combine these in certain ways to do certain things, and this is precisely what TapTurk does, but you are oversimplifying the situation to describe it as such. Again, the currency is decentralized, so there's nothing we can do at this point. This is why we want to move to a centralized chain, in which case we would be able to, for lack of a better word, censor certain transactions that seem to have anti-social objectives. Everything that happens on TapTurk happens on Bounties, but not vice versa. So much of what happens on Bounties had nothing to do with TapTurk. Yes, people may have cloned some of the contracts and used them illicitly, but that is beyond my control. I say adamantly and repeat, everything Tapboard has done has been within the bounds of the law. If you would like to change the law, that, fortunately is under your purview. We operate under strict accordance with the law.

SILVA : Tapboard is not on trial here. We are trying to protect democracy. Are you aware that a bounty was created leading to the assassination of a Chinese national named Da?

GREYWAHL : Yes. I'm aware of that. This bounty was specifically engineered without really anything to do with Tapboard or TapTurk. We don't know a lot about that. I have nothing to add to that.

SILVA : Fair enough. Let's move away from the payment of the bounties. I'm hearing that you don't have anything to say about this because the payments did not go via your gigging network, TapTurk. But what did happen on Tapboard? Millions of posts with deliberate misinformation were posted and shared. Perhaps these were motivated by payments that you did not control, but they were made in Tapcoin and to Tapboard users for the explicit purpose of actions that were undertaken on Tapboard. That's why you're here.

GREYWAHL : OK, but free speech is free speech. Lying is free speech. Free speech is the law of the land. I know you don't like it, but paid speech is free speech. Money is free speech, and I'm sure that applies to cryptocurrency as well as dollars. We can't possibly step in and fact-check every post that makes its way onto Tapboard.

SILVA : Sorry, I should ask you a more specific question. You're not on trial. When I ask the question, I'm not trying to score points or ask a rhetorical question, I, we, the committee, want to know. How did this happen?

GREYWAHL : With all due respect, that's not a very specific question.

SILVA : Let's go through this slowly. Explain to me like I'm 80. The people who shared this information. Were they targeted specifically?

GREYWAHL : Targeted?

SILVA : Clearly, they were paid. So at some point someone had to make a solicitation: "hey I'll pay you $500 to share this meme containing misinformation."

GREYWAHL : I'm guessing the answer is "yes." We feature promoted ads, that do advertise bounties to users, even when the bounties are external. So it's possible, likely, in fact, that there were advertisements for bounties or bounty aggregators promoted to our users.

SILVA : But were they targeted specifically?

GREYWAHL : You mean to ask if the ads made use of standard analytical tools available in order to promote the advertisements to only a subset of users? Yes, that's standard.

SILVA : How were they targeted?

GREYWAHL : Broadly speaking, AI. I won't go into our neural net architecture but it's easy to predict which users are going to respond to a given promotion. If you advertise with us, we will only direct your advertisement to parties we feel have a reasonable chance of responding.

SILVA : But how are these people selected?

GREYWAHL : It's deep learning. It's not like there's 15 variables and we use linear regression. We feed the entire user history, megabytes of data per user, into a very sophisticated neural network and this gives us 140 variables associated to each user. We use these variables to predict the response to each ad.

SILVA : So what do these variables correspond to? Race? Religion? Political views?

GREYWAHL : These variables are the result of what's called unsupervised learning. They have no explicit connection. You may call them "latent variables". It's possible that many of these variables correspond to various traits, but we make no attempt to discern this, because it doesn't shed any light on their predictive power. Their predictive power is in their faithfulness to the real underlying latent variables.

SILVA : And the entire user history, I assume this includes all Tapcoin transactions.

GREYWAHL : Naturally, yes.

SILVA : So you are taking users' financial records and selling these to advertisers?

GREYWAHL : What. No. Where did you get that? We plug the financial data into our own internal neural network and use the output to offer our advertising partners better matches. We don't sell the data itself.

SILVA : So advertisements are sent to users according to some 140 variables that we have, I understand, no idea what these variables mean?

GREYWAHL : You can say it like that, if you like, perhaps, but it's really much more anodyne. These variables simply are used as a quick way to judge how a user will respond to an advertisement, so that we can choose which promoted advertisements to place on their timeline. The 140 variables are simply a reduction of their entire Tap history. It's how we run so efficiently. There is a hidden "marketplace" were we solve a sort of matching problem in which advertisements are placed on users' timelines most likely to respond favorably, but keeping in mind the fact that we can't pump 100's of advertisements to one user at a time. It's a delicate matching problem. Our learned variables play a crucial role. We want to create a win-win for both our advertisers and our users. Beyond that, these variables inform our TapTurk matching algorithms. Over the years we've watched the mean rating for gig workers move up slowly from 4.1 to 4.97. This is largely because we are placing gig workers in positions were they are likely to succeed.

SILVA : Does this marketplace involve advertising space going to highest bidder?

GREYWAHL : Of course it does, it's a marketplace. We're a business, not a charity. You can describe what business does in these terms all day, but that's how free markets work. Users with variables lying in certain regions are more coveted by some advertisers, and advertising space is finite. We have been a bastion of efficiency and the grease in the economic boom. The combination of our sophisticated advertising algorithms, our marketplace, and TapTurk have created an unprecedented explosion of efficiency. Corporations have been able to make use of the global network of underemployed workers with a rich variety of skills. This was never possible before. This economically-priced labor has allowed corporations to flourish in a way previously unimaginable, and has helped accomplish one of our long stated goals: the banking of the unbanked. This banking of the unbanked is only possible when we allowed the unbanked a place on the grid. Our algorithms do this efficiently. Legacy banking played gatekeeper with their use of old-fashioned methods such as credit scores. Our 140 variables have much better predictive power. This is the result of the free market in action. Bidding, as you say, is the process which, among other things, has kept labor prices affordable and profits high. The competitive marketplace allows a corporation to hire 2-3 times as many workers as they did before, for the same price. And it allows people in traditionally underbanked groups the opportunity to gain access to the same financial system the rest of us have. This is efficiency. It's a beautiful thing.

SILVA : Do you sell information about Tapboard users?

GREYWAHL : 'Information' can mean many things, but in any case, the law does not forbid this. We don't sell individual identifiable information, but we sell aggregate information - some of this to the highest bidder on a marketplace. There is an existing and developing market for blockchain analytics products and we fill this void. Again, we don't sell individual identifying information, we sell data that corresponds to the user type and behavior.

SILVA : Do you sell this information to anybody?

GREYWAHL : No, just those with the ability to pay.

SILVA : Do you keep a record of who buys this information?

GREYWAHL : Only when required by law. Typically selling aggregate information is unrestricted.

SILVA : Now do you keep a record of the advertisements? We want to know who paid for the political ads.

GREYWAHL : In the case of political ads, we are required by law to keep a record of all political ads to ensure compliance with the FEC. This is on file with the FEC and our attorneys are happy to give this to you at a moment's notice. However, for what you're asking about, I will save you the trouble: these are ads to external websites. These external websites are not themselves political, but are venues for political websites. So we are not required to keep a record of who these advertisers are. If you include websites that have links to websites that do political things, then I guess everything is political. But we follow all FEC statutes to a 'T'.

SILVA : So the advertisements themselves are not political, but are instead advertisements for users to click through to a website which may then encourage them to engage in politics?

GREYWAHL : Essentially, in the political cases, yes. It's not direct advertising, so we aren't required to keep records.

SILVA : So do you keep records?

GREYWAHL : We do, but perhaps not the kind you'd be looking for. We catalog advertisers by a unique ID. But unless required by law we don't record the identity of anyone who pays for advertising, so usually we can't tell you to whom the ID belongs.

SILVA : Wait, what about AML/KYC laws?

GREYWAHL : These only apply when we are actually the custodial holder of coins for someone else. There's no reason we have to keep information on every counterparty in the ecosystem.

SILVA : So once again, is there anything you can tell us about the use of Tapboard for perpetuating disinformation leading to the most recent election fiasco?

GREYWAHL : Again, this was Tapboard users exercising their free speech in large. They were paid in Tapcoin, but because Tapcoin is a decentralized protocol, I can't speak to that. What I can tell you is that with unpermissioned payment networks, unscrupulous anonymous players have gained control of various parts of the networks. This is something you as regulators need to deal with before it is completely out of your hands, if it is not too late already. If you think Tapcoin and Alice are too big to regulate, I wouldn't recommend waiting around for better opportunities.

Without a central authority, it's always a shell game to push around the security flaw. But the secret is that there is no security flaw. When the system is working as it's supposed to, it's basically insecure. You can cover this up with some inefficiency or another, but ultimately if you have enough weight you can control the system, and answer to no one. This ecosystem needs central authority to function efficiently. Perhaps you've heard the folklore theorem: A decentralized, permissionless system cannot be both efficient and secure. Free market forces plus smart contract efficiency always break down the security barriers, with a little bit of leverage.

You can come to me and ask about the free speech that happened on my network, but it's the unregulated financial system to blame, the system that many of you in this room signed up for a few years back when you agreed to deregulate the industry. Blaming free speech is not the solution. But I feel like we've had this conversation before. You can't expect to control free speech, especially if it's defined by money. If you want to keep a thumb on dangerous and inappropriate speech, you have to control the money. As long as we have decentralized payment systems and money is speech we have this sort of problem.

SILVA : OK. This is noted. Not to misrepresent the record, but you were here in the earlier part of the decade, advocating strongly for rapid deregulation.

GREYWAHL : I think I've grown and learned a lot. I apologize for my neglect to consider the consequences of deregulation.

SILVA : Do you have any way to tell us who the major holders of Tapcoin are? For example, would you be able to give me a list of parties that own more than $100 billion in Tapcoin?

GREYWAHL : Again, this is a decentralized anonymous currency. I can't tell you that information, because I have no way to determine it precisely, at least anymore than anyone else does.

SILVA : OK. So we don't know who was behind this. What measures can you take so that disinformation doesn't spread so rapidly, say next Tuesday?

GREYWAHL : At this point, very little. Like I said we have a partially decentralized architecture - it was built to be censorship resistant. We didn't want any government to tell us to stop free speech, and by essentially taking away our ability to do this, we can tell any would-be Ministry of Truth that, sorry, there's nothing we can do, you have to turn off the internet.

SILVA : So if misinformation begins spreading rapidly there's nothing you can do.

GREYWAHL : We can't turn off the internet. We have worked with established agencies to set up and publicize channels so that legitimate information is being shared. But you know people. If you try to censor misinformation, it only makes it more enticing to share. We just hope there is more general awareness now.

SILVA : Can you tell me if QR overlays were used in some of the disinformation memes?

GREYWAHL : Indeed, this is common practice.

SILVA : How did this work?

GREYWAHL : Each meme that is shared has a QR overlay - this contains a payment code and a often a contract code so these can be harvested by miners.

SILVA : Tapboard provides an API for this?

GREYWAHL : We do.

SILVA : I have no further questions, thank you.

CHAIR : OK, thank you. The chair recognizes Senator Reese.

REESE : OK. I want to go back a bit. Da. As we mentioned, Da was assassinated recently. You also mentioned that Da and Paul Preston had orchestrated an attack on the Bitcoin blockchain. Do you believe there is any connection here?

GREYWAHL : It's quite possible. I don't want to speculate too much.

REESE : Da, Chinese, right?

GREYWAHL : I believe so.

REESE : But not really in good graces with the Chinese?

GREYWAHL : Da is known as a free speech activist who speaks out against the Communist Party. Da has been in hiding for years.

REESE : And then, last month he shows up dead. Would the Chinese government have done this? If so why did they wait?

GREYWAHL : I agree with what I think you're implying. The Communist Party would never have killed him and dumped his body on the streets after he's been such a vocal outspoken activist. They would be better off making sure he disappears. The last thing they want is a free speech martyr.

REESE : Unless he was about to exercise free speech and blow the cover off of something big?

GREYWAHL : Again, same principle, they would be wiser dispatching him in secret.

REESE : But what if that's not possible? What if they can't catch him and whisk him off - they just have to take him out and deal with the risk. They certainly have the funds to create the assassination bounty.

GREYWAHL : If you're suggesting that Da knew something he shouldn't and there was no choice - I think I could buy that explanation.

REESE : How is your relationship with China?

GREYWAHL : We, Tapboard, don't have the market penetration we would like. They (the party) don't really like us, but we don't have a relationship, so to speak. Because the architecture is partially decentralized it's somewhat hard for them to negotiate directly with us and make certain demands like they have with tech firms in the past.

REESE : Have you met Da?

GREYWAHL : I have not.

REESE : Have you communicated with Da?

GREYWAHL : Yes, quite often. When James Andrews, my cofounder left Tapboard years ago, he sold his shares to Jing first and then some to Da.
These two ended up being sort of savage enemies over the years, always
lobbying for different outcomes.

REESE : Have you met Jing? Communicated with Jing?

GREYWAHL : I never met Jing. Jing was a little strange in that he doesn't do
person-to-person so much. He prefers to post online and wax philosophical
about every decision. Despite being sort of a master trader and market
mover, Jing isn't that transactional. So I never had a one-on-one with
Jing. He owns or has owned at one point probably 60% of the shares, but
he's mostly hands off.

REESE : Is Jing political? An activist?

GREYWAHL : I don't know if that's true. That's going around for sure, there's
a lot of conspiracy theories surrounding him, but in my interaction I don't
get a strong whiff of political leanings.

REESE : Did Jing ever weigh in on Tapboard's policies regarding, say, fact
checking or; for lack of a better word, censoring, posts on Tapboard?

GREYWAHL : Jing wasn't especially vocal here, but had a very basic insistence
that we don't censor and that free speech should always be the rule.

REESE : Did Jing participate in the attack on Bitcoin?

GREYWAHL : I don't believe he participated as much as let it happen and
took advantage of it. Like I said he has an uncanny ability to time the
market, which is probably not uncanny after all - I think he has some
information about what's going down before everyone else does. In this
case in particular, Jing shorted Bitcoin at precisely the right time. He
made a post about this claiming he didn't have any personal feelings about
the attack but you have to dance when the music plays. He didn't bother
to say how he would have learned about this. But I think his string of

successful market plays is as much insider information as anything else. Obviously someone leaked something about it.

REESE : Is Jing directly affiliated with the Chinese Communist Party?

GREYWAHL : I don't have knowledge there.

REESE : If you were to name an individual, group or nation who did this, who would you point fingers at?

GREYWAHL : Nothing jumps clearly into my mind and I don't care to speculate beyond that.

REESE : China? Yes?

GREYWAHL : Again I don't care to speculate.

REESE : I have no further questions.

5

TESTIMONY OF THE FIRST WITNESS, part II. Mr. Paul Preston, CEO, EWD Consultants, LLC.

CHAIR : Good Morning. Mr. Preston has agreed to return to finish his testimony. Ranking Member Silva has the floor.

SILVA : Can you tell me about some of the work you've done with China?

PRESTON : So again, I've never been invited in any official capacity to do anything with China, per se. I have done work with Da, who seemed to have a lot of cryptocurrency and let on that perhaps he had connections.

SILVA : Da. Great. Is Da an agent of the Chinese government?

PRESTON : No, but he occasionally claimed, or at least suggested that he had some relations to them. I never pushed, but he made it sound like his father or uncle was an important top-level player.

SILVA : OK. We'd like to talk about your relationship with Da. Have you actually met Da?

PRESTON : Da was a somewhat mysterious character. I think I've only met him once. Many years ago, when no one knew who he was, he approached me at a crypto conference in Tokyo and tried to strike up a conversation. We started up an email correspondence after that.

SILVA : So Da is (or was?) a real person?

PRESTON : I assumed so - I mean, I met some guy named Da and then I started emailing him soon after, I don't know what else Da could be.

SILVA : What is his nationality?

PRESTON : I assume Chinese. He looked Chinese - and I work in Singapore
    so I can actually tell the difference between Chinese, Japanese, Korean,
    Vietnamese, etc without a problem - and I seem to remember him speaking
    in Mandarin to other people comfortably. Always using a word I won't
    repeat, the one that starts with an 'n' and rhymes with "zhege." In fact I
    tried to speak Mandarin with him, and he seemed to get some of it, but
    insisted on speaking English. His English wasn't good at all. It was better
    than my Mandarin though, so that's what we used. Email and Tapboard
    worked much better.

SILVA : Can you describe him?

PRESTON : Young, shy, with spazzy bursts of confidence. His English was not
    good, but also I wouldn't be surprised if he was 16 or 17 when I met him.
    He wore this bulky Chicago Bulls parka from like 1991, even though it was
    warm in Tokyo. Kind of a nervous jumpy dude. Shorter, probably not
    even five feet tall.

SILVA : Was he a political figure himself?

PRESTON : I don't think he was a politician, if that's what you're asking. Like I
    said I think he was a kid when I met him. He was both a master trader and
    a technical guru, but from what I can tell not political at all. I also guessed
    that because he seemed like a kid that could do anything he wanted with
    his time, that most likely, he came from some sort of privileged upbringing.
    He was always looking for angles and inefficiencies in the cryptocurrency
    itself, as well as the markets. That being said I don't know him too well.
    Who knows. I never asked him.

SILVA : I guess, maybe a big question about Da is "is he alive?"

PRESTON : That's a very good question. As you probably know there was a
    very strangely written bounty put on his head. The price was $16 billion or
    something. This was paid out, which means someone confirmed it. There
    were pictures posted of an accident scene and someone that looked like

him - but you know, deepfakes and all I wouldn't trust a picture. What we do know is that the bounty was confirmed, resolved, and paid. If he wasn't dead I would think this would be contested.

SILVA : Before we go into the specifics of this bounty, do you know who would want him dead?

PRESTON : Well. Lots of people. It's a nasty space.

SILVA : Indulge me.

PRESTON : How to narrow down this question.

SILVA : We have all day. What jumps into your mind?

PRESTON : It's sort of a sensitive, also long story.

SILVA : Well, perhaps you already are aware. Many of the accounts that submitted the election bounties also profited off the assassination of Da. Obviously, if we can figure out who wanted Da dead we may have an idea who is behind all of the election mischief.

PRESTON : Yes, very good. I think we're on the same page.

SILVA : So? We're trying to understand. Are these mercenaries or malicious state actors? What's going on here?

PRESTON : OK. So you said you have all day. Da is complicated - he was part of the operation to take down Bitcoin, as was I. In fact you could say that Da was the leader of the attack on Bitcoin. In the process he has accumulated some bitter enemies. He's also a major holder of Tapcoin, Alice, as well as a few other coins. As a major holder myself, I have to often ask myself these questions, you know, who would want him, or myself, dead.

SILVA : I'd like to return to this Bitcoin operation at length, but briefly, can you give me your thoughts on the latter concern?

PRESTON : Since Da was assassinated, actually, since well before Da was assassinated, but in much more urgency since then, I've taken a number of precautions - expensive security, obviously, a detail with some pretty sweet weaponry, but I also have closely guarded plans to redistribute my holdings if anything were to happen to me. This is what's called an executor network. It's run by smart contracts on several blockchains. The point is that you don't want to give anyone incentive to take you out. If you own a coin that is of short supply, say you own 20% of a coin, because you founded it or something - and someone kills you, your passwords and everything might go to oblivion with you. If the keys are lost, then, in essence, that much of the coin is destroyed, and it becomes much more scarce. This often creates a nonlinear change in the price. So it's possible that destroying the major holder of a coin can increase the value of the remaining holders. For what it's worth, people used to believe that killing, say, a founder of a coin would hurt the coin, but, after there were death scares and rumors a few years back it became clear the opposite was in effect. So what we often do is engineer a contract such that if I don't check in or transact from my private keys, there's a set of executors (1000s of accounts, but I only know how many are real and how many are dummy or dead accounts) that execute instructions. These chime in, via a smart contract, and if it's clear I'm not OK, my money gets distributed. Some people take this further and use dark layers, but I don't think I need that for my security. Now you don't know how much will be distributed, how much will be destroyed - somewhere in between 0 and and 100%. But you do know that you don't know what to expect by killing me. I don't distribute all of it - if I did that you would want to short it before taking me out. There's actually a random component built into the contract, with some very precise parameters chosen. You also know my wife doesn't have any keys, so no need to hassle her. There's no clear profit play off my death. That's one measure of security. This doesn't rule out irrational reasons like revenge, however.

SILVA : So you're saying that some fraction of your coin will be redistributed if you die?

PRESTON : Exactly. At least those tied to supply and demand markets. The stablecoins go to my heirs and charitable foundations in a more predictable way. I don't disclose that number, or to whom, but yes. I wouldn't want to give anybody any ideas.

SILVA : Was this the case with Da?

PRESTON : It appears no. Surprisingly. I don't see any evidence of this - and believe me we looked. However, the strange thing is that he seemed to see the threat coming and transfered his coins to some different accounts before he died. It's unclear why, it could be because he saw the bounty spike and figured he was a deadman. I don't know to whom he would have transfered it. These accounts haven't moved since he supposedly died.

SILVA : So you don't think he was murdered just for financial incentives - I mean someone would have to make a lot of money on some financial instrument in order to pay the $16 Billion bounty, right?

PRESTON : I agree with your assessment.

SILVA : So the other possibility was revenge. Do you know who would be out to get him?

PRESTON : Da and I were among the main catalysts for crashing Bitcoin, I guess to be fair, there were others who participated. But I think people knew he was involved in this - it was no major secret in the community. So it's possible that this may have really angered someone, and they finally exacted their comeuppance. It's a nasty game.

SILVA : OK, lead me through a little bit more of this. The media describes that Tapcoin sort of made Bitcoin irrelevant, that Bitcoin had gone out of fashion, and that there had been a few major attacks on the network. I imagine there's a backstory here?

PRESTON : Well, we hire some of the world's most fantastic PR people - these are precisely the narratives we wanted the media to pick up. Behind the scenes there was absolutely a concerted effort. Long story, but you asked. It's also a good story, something I'm proud of, and something that only a few people have really figured out. You have a few minutes?

SILVA : We have all week. Shoot.

PRESTON : OK. I met Da at a conference in Tokyo - this is about 7 years ago. He walks up to me and introduces himself, says, he's thinks Ricci is great etc, and then shoves what I think is a whitepaper in my face, and says something, like "Do you know what this means?" but his English was poor. So I thought this was another whitepaper pitch, and was looking over him, literally, and he keeps insisting I look at the paper. I finally hear him repeating "this will end Proof of Work" at which point I look down and see that it's not your standard ICO whitepaper pitch, but an academic article - I could see the arXiv paper number along the side - so I figured this was something with math or computer science. The paper was about encryption and deep learning, and something called Komolgorov Complexity. I glanced at it briefly and didn't see exactly how this was supposed to cripple Bitcoin, and Da says "I explain to you, I explain to you" and I began to see what he was trying to say: Artificial intelligence turns trillions of disconnected collections of data into actionable human knowledge. The consumers and producers of AI could pay miners for computer time, and if the conditions are right, they may pay even more handsomely than the market for mined Bitcoins. At this point I was intrigued, because I knew instantly what he was getting at: For years, probably the most common defense of Proof of Work as a security mechanism is the idea that no miners would ever allow themselves to be compromised, because they would be shooting themselves in the foot. This is in response to the suggestion that had been made for years that, why don't people just bribe miners, more than the block reward. The canned answer that everyone seemed to give was that these miners had outlayed thousands or millions in mining rigs and weren't about to sell out their ecosystem - they want it to be there longterm. Why shoot the cow for meat when you're making good money selling the milk? Longterm self-interest beats short-term self-interest. Now, it seems that if there is some economic means of making their investment in mining hardware payoff in other ways, suddenly there is less incentive for them to be loyal to the ecosystem, and all bets are off.

Now personally, I've always had strongly ambivalent feelings on Bitcoin.

Of course, I made my first millions and made a name for myself with it, but then again, I'm not loyal to it. The problem, and this is a problem that by now I think most people are aware of, is that Proof of Work is extremely wasteful. Immorally wasteful. There's no good reason just to be burning up electricity, polluting the environment, with so much human suffering for lack of resources. It's unconscionable. One of the main reasons I founded Ricci was to offer an alternative that wasn't so disgustingly wasteful.

SILVA : OK, so could you explain this a little more, I think you explained this earlier, but I don't think I understood it 100%. Proof of Work?

PRESTON : I don't think I explained it in any detail before. It's slightly involved, but here goes. So the blockchain is an ordered set of blocks. People can create transactions and broadcast these, but these don't become actual transactions until someone, that someone being a miner, writes them on the next block. So if I want to send you Bitcoins, I sign a note, with my cryptographic digital signature, saying, I'm sending Silva 15 Bitcoins. I send this out there. Now, for this actually to happen, someone needs to verify this transaction is good, that my key is correct, that I have the funds to spend, that your address is valid, etc, and so they do that, they being the minors, and they do this at the same time for a whole bunch of other transactions. They put these together and call it a block - just think of this as a page full of valid transactions that don't contradict any previous transactions. Now the reward for writing a block is a lot of money, in order to keep people incentivized to write the blocks. But you also have to make it hard, or everyone would be writing blocks at the same time, and there would be no consensus. So the genius of Satoshi was to come up with a system that uses probability to decide who gets to write the next block, in a way that will be fair, and will be more likely to reward the miners who are spending the most electricity. Electricity and computer cycles are a finite resource. It works something like the following: you come up with your block of transactions. You then pick a large random number - this is called a nonce - and you hash the block, seeded with your nonce. In other words, this is just a very involved mathematical computation that spits out a number, and this output number is very hard to predict. If you change the nonce by 1, you get a totally different output. So basically the number coming out of this computation is pretty much random, but depends on the nonce you give it. So the agreement is that the first person to find a nonce, hash the block and have an output that is very small, this person gets to write the block. The odds are tough - just to make up some numbers, you have pick a number in between 1 and 10 Trillion and this number gets hashed in an unpredictable way, and spits out another number between 1 and 10 trillion, and if the number is less than, say 200, you win, unless of course someone else got to a number lower than 200 before you did, and they won. But the odds of this are very low each time you hash the numbers. However, you are using a powerful computer, so you can do these computations many times a second. Something that has a one in a million chance of succeeding, if you repeat this 10,000 times, the chance of succeeding is now roughly around 1%. So if everybody around the world is playing this same lottery, we expect that someone will win after a few minutes. Once this person gets this winning lottery ticket, the block is theirs, and everybody starts trying to write the next block. Now, of course you might ask, what if two people write the block, roughly at the same time? Well that's a very good question, and the answer is, the other miners decide independently which block to append to. Some miners may append a block to one chain, some may append a block to the other. The rule is the longest chain wins. So once word gets around that there's a longer chain, other miners will start trying to write on the longest chain. If you write a block to a chain that doesn't get included, you've just wasted your energy and you don't get the block reward.

SILVA : Why is it called Proof of Work? Where's the proof? and what's the work?

PRESTON : Perhaps this isn't the best term, because it can be misleading. Being a mathematician I can tell you it's not like a mathematical proof. It's more like, evidence of work. The idea is that you probably won't have found a way to come up with the right numbers, unless you've tried thousands or millions of possibilities. It's not a 100% proof that you spent a lot of energy, rather, the odds that you picked the right seed at random before trying thousands of possibilities is extremely low. So, no, it's not a proof. But coming up with the right number strongly suggests you've invested some energy in the process. The work refers to all of the computer cycles you ran. Ultimately, if you are using 2% of the computer cycles in the world who are attempting to mine Bitcoin at this very moment, you have a 2% chance of creating the next block. This is how it can be equitable and decentralized.

SILVA : OK. This is, fascinating. I think I'm understanding, so it's sort of a race to plug the right numbers into a formula?

PRESTON : More or less, yes, and the more powerful computer you have the more equipped you are to win the race.

SILVA : Well thank you Mr. Preston. This is one of the more comprehensible explanations I've been given. I think I understand how this could cause a lot of computer power to be spent.

PRESTON : Very good. You see what's going on - if everybody's goal is to produce thousands of hashes to get the next reward, you end up with this situation where millions of hashes are being produced every minute all around the world, and it's sort of a big waste of energy. People were OK with this for awhile, actually many still are, but after years of this it became clear to many of us that this was just dumb and inefficient. There were a number of ideas floating around, and one of the ones that was most reasonable was something called "Proof of Stake". The idea of Proof of Stake is that instead of having people that have nothing to do with the network compete to write a block based on raw computing power, you have people that have some stake in the network write the block. In particular, only the coin holders can write the next block. It's of course a bit more complicated than this, and I'm happy to go into it, but the game theory follows from the idea that you aren't going to work to frustrate a network that you have an investment in. The big advantage is that most implementations don't require an ungodly amount of computer cycles. So, I hope I've convinced you why I was morally opposed to Proof of Work, in fact I remember thinking that if someone can get people to abandon Proof of Work for other consensus methods, this person deserves a Nobel Peace Prize. So I was intrigued when Da was telling me that we could cripple it. We started an email interaction, or I guess, mostly chatted over Tapboard. He had a channel set up, and there were 5 users total in the channel. We spoke pretty openly about our goals. I wanted to see Bitcoin thrown in the dumpster and I wanted Ricci to take over and see Alice take it's spot as the world's top currency. Da wanted to make money, so did the others involved, and it seemed they had a lot of it to throw around to get the process started.

SILVA : Do you know who these other people were?

PRESTON : Actually, no. I never asked because it seemed like if they wanted me to know, they would tell me. Da knew them, apparently, and had given them handles of Ross, Joey and Chandler - apparently he had learned English by watching a bunch of 90's TV on TapFlix. So that's how I know them. Chandler apparently was some sort of a whale, he had a lot of funds, like billions of US Dollars worth, on a number of exchanges. Ross knew the Bitcoin core software extremely well, and Joey had some sort of marketing prowess on social media and access to some guerrilla marketing firms. I don't know how Da knew all these people, but he assured me that he had put together sort of a dream team and had a pretty good outline of a plan that would be in our shared interests. I was on the team for two reasons - first, I had a lot to gain if my chain were to overtake Bitcoin, this along with the fact that I had long been outspoken against Proof of Work, this led Da to believe I was a pretty surefire ally. This was right, but they also wanted me to use the Ricci protocol to make sure that Bounties were working in a way that would facilitate miners switching off the Bitcoin blockchain and toward machine learning opportunities that were being payed out in Alice. They needed a mechanism for miners to easily profit while not mining. I was all in. Our plan was to weaken the Proof of Work difficulty in the Bitcoin blockchain, to the point where we could create a secret fork, run this fork parallel for several days, and then lengthen the fork beyond that of the main chain by brute force, and foist it on the network. Now I was skeptical, I mean, at first when Da showed me the paper about deep learning I had been excited, but when I went home and thought about it I was less excited. So when he put the group together-

SILVA : I apologize, I'm still trying to process this - foist a fork on the network? Proof of Work difficulty? Is this something you can explain in laymen terms?

PRESTON : Sure. This is classical stuff from cryptocurrency, but you guys in this room spend all your time trying to regulate things instead of designing them, so I guess I get explain these terms. That's fine.

First, difficulty. Each block is supposed to take ten minutes to be mined. This is just an average. Because it's a Poisson process, it might take 4 minutes now, 12 minutes next block, 21 minutes next block 8 minutes, etc, but over a period of a week or so it's supposed to average out to ten minutes per block. When the price goes high, more miners jump in, and start dedicating more computing power in order to chase the block reward. This decreases the expected time, proportional to the increase in price. So what happens is that every so often, the blockchain recalibrates the difficulty. Suppose say, that the chances that a given hash you're about to produce will win the block are say 1 out of a million. Now if the price doubles, it's reasonable that twice as much power will be chasing the block, so the solution is to drop the difficulty by an equivalent factor. Now the chances of creating a winning block is 1 out of 2 million per hash. So if miners start to drop out of the pool, the blocks can start to take a bit longer, and the blockchain recalibrates the difficulty. So our goal was to slowly push this difficulty out a bit so that when we applied our full power, we would be able to write blocks at say an average of 8 minutes per block. Perhaps I should go back a bit and re-emphasize an earlier point. Recall this Bitcoin blockchain is a series of blocks containing Bitcoin transactions, a series as in hundreds of thousands. Each block in the chain points to the previous block, so these have a definite ordering, each block has a number. Block 7012 comes after block 7011, etc. Now the rule is in order to write the next block, you have to come up with a good hash, which usually requires a lot of work and some luck, but there's one very important rule for making it absolutely certain which block comes next, and that is, the longest chain, that is, the chain with the most blocks, is the valid chain. I explained this two minutes ago but this is important. If the chain is N blocks long, and two miners both create block N+1 at the same time, then they are both potentially valid, for a moment at least. This is called a fork. Usually, when some other miner mines a block N+2, they have to pick which chain they are incrementing, at this point the other miners will usually jump to the longest chain. If they don't jump to the longest chain, and choose instead to write a block on a lesser fork, they run the risk of the block they write becoming orphaned, that is, nobody cares if you wrote a block that was on the wrong chain. Basically, the game is follow the front runner or get left out. Now in theory, a fork could go on for a while, but it would be hard to maintain this because usually miners will want to quickly decide which fork is going to win, that way no one wastes computer cycles mining the wrong chain. Short term forks are always possible, and this is often why transactions are said to be confirmed when 6 blocks pass - it's because it would be extremely improbable for miners to create a fork 6 blocks back, have that catch up, and then have this fork become the valid chain. The security issue that this solves is the double-spend problem. The name describes it well, but just to be pedantic: Suppose I sent you $10,000 and then tomorrow I send the same $10,000 to someone else. Now I have my own private keys, and I can sign a transaction saying, "that $10,000 I had as of yesterday morning, send it to so-and-so" even though I already sent it to you. Now you want to make sure that this didn't happen. The only way I could execute such a double spend is if I basically was able to erase the transaction I sent to you, and somehow get everyone to think that I sent the funds to this other person before I sent it to you. I can't actually invalidate the transaction in which I sent it to you, because that's a valid transaction at least according to cryptography, but what I can do is make it incompatible with other transactions that are also valid. This becomes improbable after a few blocks pass.

So our plan was to wait until a moment when the chain was significantly weak, and then start creating our own fork - basically just mine transactions on our own for a while, in secret. We would send ourselves a bunch of transactions that contradicted transactions we had sent to exchanges around the world, and been credited for. Then after several days, we would broadcast the fork. The rules are the rules, and the longest chain wins. This was, of course, easier said than done and took some planning. This wasn't our idea completely - several times in the past when various hacks had taken place, people would suggest a 'reorg', which is a more political term for a fork. This is just a way of motivating miners to write to a different chain.

Getting back to your question, yes, we just wanted to create a longer chain than the previously accepted one, and a chain that differed from a few days back. This would cause maximal confusion and hopefully despair among those who thought that Proof of Work was an infallible security mechanism.

My main role in the process was to facilitate, for as many miners as possible, a repurposing of cycles toward neuromining, as we called it. This was executed in two parts. One involved setting up Bounties to buy the cycles, and the other was to develop some academic research suggesting that neuromining was feasible and enterprise viable. I'll talk about the latter and then go back to the Ricci component. At the time, neuromining wasn't really accepted as a thing. There was this paper that Da showed me, but to be honest, it was kind of a word salad, not really easy to read. The introduction was clear, I could see the idea, but I wasn't sure about the details. Now like I said earlier, one of the applications of Bounties was to mobilize computing power throughout the world to perform heavy machine learning tasks. We hadn't intended to use actual mining rigs. It's a completely different type of floating point GPU type computation necessary for the deep learning, compared to crypto mining. So there was some loose link, but my feelings at first were that there wasn't a solid way to utilize ASICS efficiently for machine learning purposes.

So I gave the paper to some of our brilliant postdocs and they sort of had the same assessment, that this paper didn't really state a clear theorem and it was hard to really say for sure if it was correct, but there was a germ of a really brilliant idea in here. Our postdocs frequently are asked to referee academic papers by some of the top journals in the field, and I encourage them to do this. Their assessment was that if they had been given this paper to referee, they would send it back with bunch of red ink saying "please explain this better." So this paper was sketchy at best. I explained this to Da, and he told me that another reason he wanted me on the job was because I was a large contributor to the research aspect of the discipline, and I could surely arrange that this paper received the proper research attention. I suggested that I could have a team of my postdocs look into it further, and he said that, no, the conflict of interest is too obvious, that we should partner up with researchers at major universities. So I reached out to a number of researchers at Carnegie Mellon, Stanford, University of Paris, Duke, Tsinghua and started some correspondences about this. Now of course, neuroming wasn't even a thing. It didn't really make sense to me or other experts. So there was no current research to further, at the time. But as I looked further, I discovered that this was actually a brilliant idea, and it might sound complicated, but if you give me a minute I can explain why this was so promising: For much of the previous decade or two Deep Learning had grown in power and scope in dramatic exponential fashion - around 2010 it was still mostly theory, by 2020, you could deep-fake or classify almost anything. This was just due to the computing power afforded by the technology available, which allowed for the stochastic gradient descent computations. Again, the goal in machine learning is usually to minimize some "loss" value in your prediction model. The SGD method only tests nearby values and re-updates, or to be precise, computes a local gradient. This was amazingly successful, for most, and by most I mean, I don't know, 98% of the problems it was applied to. But the more interesting, and more vexing problems just didn't seem to find the best answers. There was a lot of chatter in the AI community in the early part of the decade about why SGD works so well - this was a mystery. You have this mystery that it works in over-parameterized models, for example. This is absurd, everybody knows that over-parameterizing a model should give you garbage but for some reason with deep learning it works great.

If you can understand why it works, you can understand why it fails. The answer that started to emerge involved this idea of Komolgorov Complexity - the idea is that most of the phenomena we observe in nature, while they appear complicated, they actually really aren't that complicated from a "how to create this" point of view. For example, if you see a fractal, you might think that a fractal is a really complicated object, but they are actually really simple to create with a computer program - you just repeat a simple rule. But you would make yourself go crazy trying to approximate a fractal with a polynomial. Nature is like that, you construct really complicated looking systems from not-so-complicated instructions. It turns out Deep Learning keys into this - the distribution of outputs of deep learning models is, about, roughly, as complicated as things that happen in nature. However, there are things that happen in nature that are on the tail end of this distribution that are really legitimately complicated - these are the very things we want most to understand, naturally. So one of the promising ideas that was emerging in the last ten years is that we can estimate the Komolgorov Complexity of certain phenomena in nature, and then you can tailor your deep learning models to search out these more complicate regimes. This requires a different kind of computer power and you can't simply use SGD floating point operations to do this, you need some pretty advanced algebraic capabilities, and these are what's provided by the mining rigs. It's much more complicated and nuanced than I just described, but slowly this picture was emerging. So we pushed it hard. Many Universities across the country were working on forming these interdisciplinary "clusters of excellence" and touting their own cutting edge research. So the newest trend in AI wasn't hard to find collaboration partners for. We set up a collaboration with pharmaceutical companies and medical labs, who used mining rigs to do things like folding proteins and finding harmful interactions between drugs. In fact, one story I was told was that one of the pharmaceutical companies had a huge neural net set up, and was able to detect that a certain interaction was fatal like 40% of the time. It was bizarre because there was no scientific explanation, but the neural net found it, and sure enough, they were able to find prescriptions of people at risk of some very dangerous complications. So this saved lives. Our project saved lives. This is real science and I'm proud of these aspects. Of course, this was actually sort of serendipity, but that's the beauty of the free market combined with academic freedom. I started working on this idea hoping for the goal of destroying Bitcoin, and what resulted is a new era in Deep Learning. Now on our end, in order to get this going, we just had to develop a built-in platform layer into Ricci, and this was actually fairly easy to do with my team of engineers. Once this functionality was set up, we sort of chummed the waters by putting out some bounties that paid a multiple of 5-10 times over what mining pools would pay. We had some cash on hand, so this worked well. Joey has a bunch of PR connections and runs a bunch of news aggregators, and was able to create a bunch of stories describing how all the Bitcoin miners were switching over to neuromining and raking in massive cash. I'll admit this was a bit of a deliberate exaggeration, but sometimes you have to prime the pump. We also put out a series of news stories, directed at the machine learning community describing how neuromining was revolutionizing the industry. We had no compunctions about name-dropping Stanford or Duke. It worked. It worked well, a number of Bitcoin miners did stop mining, and they actually did end up performing a lot of important machine learning work. Now this is noble, I'm quite proud of this to this day - some people probably are still furious at me for redirecting cycles away from Bitcoin, but I'm proud of this. I've gotten more than my share of death threats, but I'd do it again.

SILVA : Excuse me for a minute, I'm not an expert in this area at all, but I've read about this, didn't this KCT turn out to be sort of a, um, fad, that never panned out?

PRESTON : A fad? Seriously, there have been over 7,000 papers posted on ArXiv with the terms Komolgorov Complexity - this is not a fad. You insult thousands of prominent Ph.D's when you say that. Yes, industry has been a little slow to catch up, this is true, but that's expected, most industry is a little bit behind the curve of the academic research. This is why I hire a team of the leading experts, so that we at EWD are not behind. But it's ludicrous to call this a fad. I already told you how this project had an impact in the pharmaceutical industry.

SILVA : Continue.

PRESTON : So this aspect was wildly successful, and we were able to devote, we guess, maybe 10-15% of the Bitcoin mining cycles away from mining Bitcoin. This wasn't quite enough, so the next thing we needed to do was crash the market. Now this was 2024. One thing we were working towards was the halving. In 2024 the block reward would drop in half, miners would be getting half of the block reward each time. So naturally, one would expect that the number of computers chasing half of the reward would drop commensurably.

SILVA : The block reward is cut in half? How often does this happen?

PRESTON : This was the original idea of Satoshi - every four years the block reward is cut in half. Because block reward is the only way Bitcoins can be created, this limits the number of Bitcoins created, from now to eternity. This means that, unlike the US Dollar, which one can print at will, Bitcoin is not inflationary. Every four years is measured in blocks - because each block happens every ten minutes, on average, after every so many blocks, the reward gets halved. Because the difficulty is computed on a rolling basis based on the time it takes to create blocks, the blocktime is calibrated to about ten minutes on average. The markets always behaved strangely around the halving, as it's not clear how much of the supply of Bitcoin comes from miners selling their newly minted coins to pay for the electricity, or just people selling their Bitcoins. We were hoping for both a market crash and a drop in difficulty. We decided the best thing to do was try to crash the market in stages, as the halving approached. Chandler said he could do this, and sure enough, he was able to put in a few sell orders and short orders and the markets dropped a little bit. It turns out, when you have a currency that really isn't tied to anything, the value of the coin really lies in a wide range and you can push it if you have a large enough part of the market. We generated money with a few huge leveraged shorts. There was a series of drops of about 5-10%. We lost some on a short squeeze, but that was OK, that was expected. Chandler was able to purchase some large quantities of Bitcoin off the exchange - at a premium - the price was undisclosed, but we paid 10-15% above market price for some OG hodler's coin, and then dumped this on the market. Prices crashed, this was somewhat predictable. We got burned in a short squeeze again, and I was questioning Chandler's promise that he could always crash the market at will. We put our heads together and decided we wanted to do something slightly more sophisticated. About 90% of the trading that props up the market is bots. So if you have enough money to throw around and discover the algorithms, you can start to front-run the bots. This much we knew, and had used against them, but we had only dropped the price about 15%. Instead of front-running the bots, the better plan is to control the bots. That is, you can engage in trading behavior that will force the bots to put downward pressure on the price. That was the fun part, really - not only can you use the historical data paired with current data that you essential create to control the bots, you can train these bots yourself. One thing I knew, but Chandler understood in a very deep way, is that most of the people out there writing trading scripts aren't really machine learning experts, they're just smart enough to write a bot that beats the market. They do a lot of stupid things like over-fitting to recent data. We took advantage of this - we had a huge collection of historical data. We isolated the market conditions preceding all of the market crashes over the previous ten years. Most of this was just sort of random behavior, it's eternally difficult to decode the signal from the noise, especially in these type of markets. The algorithms people were using are based on the idea that somewhere, in all the millions of data points, there's some indicator that the market's going to spike or crash, and if your model can find it, this gives you an advantage. So what we did was simply recreated these conditions as closely as possible. We can do this because we had enough accumulated in the exchanges. It's more complicated and lies under the surface, but to give you an example, many traditional investors believe in something called a double bottom or a double top - if the price of an asset increases to a certain value, then decreases, then returns to that peak before decreasing again, the common understanding is that this is "hard ceiling" and that there's no hope of ever breaching that price point anytime soon. This causes a lot of people to sell. Historically, this is borne out in a number of markets. Most market index crashes, say, the Dow or whatever, when you see this double top. It always seems to portend the end of a bull market. Now if you have enough to actually control the price, you could artificially create a double top - just to kill a bull market if you so please. This is easy - price is very sensitive. You start buying a bunch until price gets to the magic number, then you sell suddenly until it drops 5% and then buy until it gets back, and then you sell again. The markets aren't thin, but they're fickle. Now crypto traders are more sophisticated, sort of, in that they don't buy into (sorry) all of this you know, "classical analysis" with the double tops and the double moons or any of these silly creative pictorial descriptions of the graph - most crypto traders simply use deep learning algorithms and don't bother staring at the shape of the graph. So it's not as simple as creating a double top, but you can be much trickier. We took all of the historical data, and trained thousands of models, each model making it's own prediction from the historical data. Then we plugged in millions of scenarios into each of these models, and picked the scenarios that the models tend to agree were bearish. Because we had enough funds, we could simply recreate these scenarios over the next week or so. The algorithms other traders were using then predicted a price plunge, and this was self-fulfilling. The beauty of this was that we were training the bots in the process. We would spend a week creating the conditions for a crash, watch it crash, and then a few weeks later, repeat the process. Many of the bots picked up on this, our extra activity was apparently detectable by the machine learning algorithms, and so whenever we started doing our thing, the market would crash even more.

So over several months, we were able to shave 55-60% of the market price, and we found what seemed sort of like a hard bottom. Now our goal was for miners to start turning off their machines, or redirecting them towards machine learning. At about this 60% mark, it turns out that only about 20% of the Bitcoin miners sent their cycles toward machine learning. Another 10% had turned off their machines, from our reading of the hash rate. We were also in the process of setting up our own mining pool, and we started paying miners incentives to join our pool. This didn't lose us much money, because we did earn some Bitcoins in the process, and it wasn't incredibly expensive. So we had cut the hash rate by about 50% and of that hash rate we controlled about 40%.

Now I should go back a bit: About 3 months after I met Da, I was contacted by someone who said that she worked for Department of Defense. She told me I needed to meet her, and that I wasn't supposed to communicate with her on the internet, apparently DoD people still don't trust the internet, but this nice woman gave me a phone, and said "this phone is for me to call you, and for you to call me." She told me that they were aware of Da's plan, and that they were "OK with it." She told me that it was actually in the US best interests, for a number of reasons, that she couldn't go into. Apparently they knew about it, and wanted it to happen. I'm pretty sure I know why, so I didn't push any questions. They said that I wasn't supposed to deviate, and I was only to contact them if something really strange came up, or if people from a certain list of aliases tried to contact me to get involved. A bit later, I get a call from this number, who tells me that we should start our fork during the series finale of Rivers, when there would be a drop in hashrate - I said "OK" and then she hung up. I tried to guess, was this a time in which a lot of bandwidth was tied up or something, but this didn't seem to make any sense. This was still a bit before the halving. We had been gunning for an attack date of around the halving. The Rivers finale was 2 weeks away, so we upped our speed and used this as a goal.

SILVA : Sorry to interrupt. Did Da and Chandler, and these other guys know you were in contact with this individual from Department of Defense?

PRESTON : Funny. I initiated a conversation and said that we should move the timeline forward, and nobody really argued with me. I gave them some good reasons, but I'm not sure that they weren't also in the loop somehow. They were like "sounds great. Let's do that." I didn't tell them the DoD was in because I didn't want to spook anybody in case that offended them for some reason. Anyways, so then, for sure, about 3 hours before the Rivers finale, we notice that the hash rate falls by about 25% for no reason at all. We had the impression there was some kind of outage in North Korea. OK, so we fired up all of our resources, and dumped a huge set of bounties to entice miners into machine learning. Da informed me that he was paying one of the Chinese mining rigs for about half of their cycles, and according to our computations, we had about 55-60% of the hashrate. We were paying through the tooth - probably $5 million/ hour, but then the price continued to fall, and even when we stopped paying so much for the bounties, we found that we had secretly built a much longer chain, much easier than we'd expected. So we held out almost a week, and at a cost of about $500 million, but when we broadcast the longer chain, as you probably all remember, it was chaos all over Bitcoin land. We had given ourselves quite a bit of funds back, but everyone else who had been trading on exchanges and doing various things was completely screwed. Some people were, some people weren't, depending on whether you had gotten coins back that someone else had credited you. Everyone was furious - this was front page news on the New York Times and Wall Street Journal, and there were lots of ideas about how to fix it, how to create a reorg, but the consensus (sorry bad pun) was that this was a 51% attack, and it would be difficult to fight it - even a hard fork where miners just all agreed to ignore the replaced blocks would be doomed to fail if the 51% persisted in attacking the chain. After about a day watching the fallout, I got a call from this lady from DoD, who asks me where I can send her secure data. She sends me a chain that is a fork of about a week before we created our fork, and it's nearly as long as ours. She tells us, start working on this, wait another week and then we foist this one onto the blockchain. Of course we dump the coins that we had already sold once onto the market, and then start adding onto this other chain, and then boom a week or two later, you have this third fork that goes even farther back. Now people were really miffed. But again the ethos was "well them's the rules" so they just went with it, and surprisingly, the price didn't crash - it fell about 50% for about a week and leveled off at about 15% of where it had been. This was strange - everyone had thought that Bitcoin was somehow sacred for it's immutability, but clearly, I guess people didn't care that much. People blamed China and North Korea, although they couldn't figure out who.

The story that somehow hit the mainstream media was that North Korea had faked an explosion at their mining facility, transported their rigs to a friendly facility in China, and then picked up the operation again - I knew this didn't add up, but this allowed us to operate as if nothing happened. Of course, it wasn't as if nothing happened. Three days later, we get contacted by Scott Greywahl, who says that they're going to use Alice as the default currency in their messaging platform, and Alice goes to the moon - 500% gain in the next month. So we got rewarded and rewarded well. However, we were confused, because after that the Bitcoin price just leveled out and didn't seem to move. I hoped it would crash. It was about 10% of all-time-high. I was happy to see that it wasn't attracting so much wasted energy, but I would've liked to see it buried forever. I realize a lot of people lost their shirts, but everyone knew, or should have known, that this was a gamble and everyone in the game was playing to win.

I suppose some of these things might sound unethical, but I personally think I should be canonized for this. I probably have the most negative carbon footprint of any person alive, and I'm proud of that. Not, by composting every other Friday, or whatever sort of green-earth theater that these other CEOs will put on. I've actually destroyed something that was threatening the planet. Cutting 90% of the price of Bitcoin effectively cuts 90% of the wasteful energy consumption.

SILVA : Well, thank you for that background, Mr. Preston, I had no idea the backstory there. I appreciate you opening up about that before the committee. I want to go back to something you left dangling. You believe Department of Defense assisted this, and you indicate you also knew why?

PRESTON : Yes, I believe this was retaliation by the US against North Korea for operation Drip Drop.

SILVA : This sounds interesting - just so we're all on the same page, fill us in on this Drip Drop operation.

PRESTON : OK. Perhaps you remember the counterfeit currency scare about 7 or 8 years ago?

SILVA : Yes.

PRESTON : This was North Korea. I mean everybody who knows anything about this knows it was North Korea. Maybe you know this. We have a lot of internal information confirming this, as I'm sure that US Intelligence does, if they're at all competent. In a nutshell, many years back North Korea had started going all in for Bitcoin. They are a country led by dictators, and it isn't so easy to maintain a dictatorship if the country doesn't have any natural resources - dictators can get away with being dictators if they have some resource like oil and have control over this. North Korea lacks this, so what they decided to do, and this wasn't a bad plan, in my opinion, was to go for some other scarce thing. So they started mining Bitcoin. They directed a huge amount of their country's electricity towards this as well as just buying it right-out with whatever money they had. It was a bold move. By hoarding it, if they could cause a sustained spike in the price, they suddenly become a nation with a little bit of wealth. It worked OK, or it was working OK, Bitcoin's value went up in fits and spurts through much of the early part of the decade. They weren't quite there yet, though. So from what we gathered, and this makes perfect sense, they started an operation in a big factory somewhere in North Korea where they tried to counterfeit US currency. Now obviously counterfeiting money isn't easy. You can't just do it in your basement with a nifty printer, there's layers of features. However, if you want to spend 18 months and $500 million, it should be reasonable to expect to mass produce a $20 bill that feels like a $20 bill, and not just one, but, you know, if you can make one, you can make millions. So by all accounts, they did that. We don't know how many they actually made. Now it doesn't matter how much money they made, what mattered to them was that they were able to create some palpable fear that the world was going to be flooded with US dollars. The·number that was floated around, deliberately, I believe was 13.1 Trillion US dollars that had been counterfeited. Now the specificity of that estimate, by my guess, is just to add credibility to an obviously fabricated number. This number appears on Tapboard in a number of forums, in some sort of coordinated way, but there's no evidence to support this. That's a ton, literally - those pallets you see full of money are on the order of $20 million dollars, so you know, you do the math, this would mean on the order of a million pallets of fake currency. So there's no way they could actually get it into the country - that wasn't the point though. I got about $20,000 in my mailbox one day. Apparently they had compiled a list of US nationals living out of the US and sent them all fat envelopes of cash - from various post offices throughout the world. There was also this famous photo, which I believe was definitely fake news, of some ship docked in Port of Seattle that had traincars full of cash. I don't know how much money was created, but by sending it throughout the world at one time, they were able to float the rumor that there was somehow 13.1 Trillion fake USD floating around the world. The point was just to FUD the US Dollar, and it worked.

SILVA : I'm sorry, to "FUD" the US Dollar. Please explain this verb.

PRESTON : Fear, Uncertainty and Doubt. Opponents of a project often engage in this, sometimes in the form of concern trolling, sometimes circulating false rumors.

The other part of the equation was that North Korea had gone long, like, leveraged long into Bitcoin. So because they had just leveraged way up, the price was already spiking a bit, and people start seeing these images of boats full of US Dollars being loaded onto trains and hearing from their friends overseas that they got $20,000 in the mail, and there was sort of a run on Bitcoin. The price went up 250% in the course of 9 days. So this is like, for North Korea like 50 times their annual GDP they made in a single week. So all of a sudden, North Korea has gone from being a shit little economy to a major contender - like on the order of France or Germany, which for a broken-down communist-state-run crapfest like North Korea, this is completely insane. And also unacceptable, I can imagine, from US policymakers' viewpoint. I work in cryptocurrency, not for the Department of State, but I can imagine that this presents a problem for the US. I get that. Because we've treated these guys like shit for decades, and now all of a sudden they have a seat at the table and are demanding some respect. Naturally, we, being the US, wanted to fix this, and get back to the previous world order. But people keep exchanging dollars for Bitcoin, and you can't shut down the free press or the internet, so what are you going to do? I should say that I'm not one of these, but a bunch of crazy hardcore cryptoanarchists hailed North Korea as a new leader (the irony, I know) and wanted to actually move there and help them build some sort of crypto-utopia.

SILVA : North Korea never admitted to this, correct?

PRESTON : No, of course not, they denied it in all their official press releases. You know how these things work. They claimed they had superior intelligence that allowed them to predict the Bitcoin demand spike, and go long, but that they would never do anything like mess with another nation's sovereign currency. But that's what corrupt states do is just lie and the only question that drives people to actually cover anything they say is really, you know, how are they going to lie today? I think most people with any sort of common sense knew what was going on, so North Korea didn't put up any solid argument. They had proved their point.

SILVA : And generated an enormous amount of wealth out of thin air, it seems.

PRESTON : Exactly. So when I was contacted by someone from the Department of Defense, I had a pretty good idea of what their motivations would be. The US had a pretty clear interest in devaluing Bitcoin just for national security issues and also it seems like in this situation you would want to send a message to other nations that attacking our currency wasn't something you can just do and get away. They also have quite a bit of resources, I would imagine. I don't know this for a fact, but I think that the US didn't get serious about keeping their own stockpiles of cryptocurrency until after Bitcoin had gotten quite big - so they were late to the game and wanted to re-level the playing field a bit.

SILVA : So you went along with this?

PRESTON : Da and I had already planned this. I'm not usually one to make allies with Department of Defense - if you know my philosophy or have watched any of my podcasts or interviews or AMA, I don't spare any words describing my opinion of you guys and your war machines - I think the nation spends way too much of the tax payer's dollars to create weapons of war - and this is completely immoral, please don't get me started - but - at this point another ally was welcomed. I'm smart enough not to fight the US Department of Defense while I'm fighting Bitcoin. I might not have great things to say about the US 100% of the time but I certainly have much less in the way of warm feelings for North Korea, and most of all, I was very opposed to this wasteful Proof of Work. So I was completely on board. If they contacted me again for something else I may or may not go along with them, as is my right, but this is something I was definitely on board with.

SILVA : OK, so there was this concerted effort to take down Bitcoin, you were involved, Da, these three, I guess "Friends" of Da, and apparently the Department of Defense. Did you ever confirm this was Department of Defense?

PRESTON : I mean, when we met in a cafe near Tsinghua she showed me a badge. It looked legit. I didn't try to follow up, to be honest. If it wasn't legit I don't know what game they would be playing, because they didn't ask for information or have us do anything that would expose the operation.

SILVA : So what we're trying to figure out here is reasons for an organization or individual who might want to take out Da. Obviously, we know North Korea would harbor some animosity. Do you care to offer an assessment of how feasible that would be?

PRESTON : My guess is that it was not North Korea. They have been all-in for Bitcoin, very one-dimensional, as far as the cryptocurrencies go. They aren't that sophisticated. I mean Drip Drop was clever, but as far as hodling coins, they just hoard Bitcoins and didn't bother with the altcoins. The Bounties contracts were written by an expert in the Ricci protocol, not just some of the off-the-shelf bounty apps that people can port and run. As far as I know North Korea has stayed away from our platform. We have a number of nodes on the TOR network and so we can often get a good idea of were IP traffic is coming from, and there's no indication of North Korea. This doesn't preclude the possibility that North Korea paid someone outside of North Korea and already in our ecosystem, or perhaps coerced them some other way. We think this was someone within our ecosystem, "our" meaning Ricci.

SILVA : Any suspects you care to mention?

PRESTON : Yes, so there's a Chinese whale, who is largely anonymous, as I've already mentioned who goes by Jing. We don't know. Jing is very good at being anonymous, very wealthy and also quite good at keeping his wealth undetected. We really have no idea how much wealth this guy has because he keeps it moving. He (or she) also knows the Ricci protocol very well.

SILVA : Anything else you'd like to tell us about Jing?

PRESTON : I have to be honest, there is very little which I actually fully definitively 100% know about Jing. You fact-checked me last time, so I'm not going there again.

SILVA : Why would Jing have animosity towards Da?

PRESTON : They are old enemies. That much I do know. Different sides of Chinese politics. Always hated each other. I never understood it, I figured it was some sort of Chinese cultural thing I'd never fully appreciate. Like Jing was the teacher and Da was the rebellious student. They had sort of a symbiosis, so I would never have thought that Da would have pushed too far, to the point that Jing would want to take him out.

SILVA : For the record, do you happen to remember the name of the officer with Department of Defense?

PRESTON : Her name was Anna Pearson.

SILVA : Wonderful, thanks. I yield back to the Chair.

6

TESTIMONY OF THE THIRD AND FOURTH WITNESSES.
Ms. Anna Pearson, Ms. Zara Jay, Department of Homeland Security.

CHAIR : This morning we have two witnesses. Ms. Anna Pearson is Under Secretary, Science and Technology, Cryptonomics Division for the Department of Homeland Security. Ms. Pearson has served a number of positions involving law enforcement, anti-terrorism, money laundering, and cyber warfare. We also have Zara Jay. Ms. Jay is an officer in Science and Technology for the Department of Homeland Security. Ms. Jay is an expert on cryptocurrency and was involved in Tapboard before moving into law enforcement. They were gracious enough to accept our invitation with about 18 hours notice.

I now recognize Senator Reese.

REESE : So Ms. Pearson, to begin, perhaps you could tell us a little bit about the history and scope of the Cryptonomics Division.

PEARSON : We are about 5 years old. At the time when the division came to be, there was a diverse collection of agents and officers working on risks posed by digital currencies. These agents and officers were found in various branches of government; Department of State, Department of Defense, Homeland Security. There were several organizations with the same intentions, specifically to promote economic behaviors that support US national policy objectives, through active and covert measures. An effort was made to consolidate these various groups under one division. As digital currencies grew to envelop a larger part of international commerce, different threat vectors began to emerge. Dictators and terrorist organizations became speculators and coinshillers, as did resistance organizations. As more digital currencies worked their way into the fiber of our economy and the economies of our trade partners, it became clear that we have a duty to maintain the stability of these payment channels against would-be attackers. We work closely with other agencies and occasionally other governments in assessing and eliminating threats. It's not uncommon to work with allies to freeze funds of suspected terrorists. We do not stand idly by while shadowy figures advance interests hostile to democracy and to the United States. On the other side of this token, these emerging vectors broaden our own abilities to advance United States' interest throughout the globe with the use of new tactics and methods.

My background is from PSYOP: as you may know the objective of PSYOP is to convey selected information and indicators to foreign audiences to influence their emotions, motives, objective reasoning, and ultimately the behavior of foreign governments, organizations, groups, and individuals. The larger purpose of psychological operations is to induce or reinforce foreign attitudes and behaviors that are favorable to the US. The vast majority of our operations are informed by my background in PSYOP and follow basic PSYOP doctrinal precepts and considerations.

REESE : You've just stated that your division has the ability to freeze funds on a blockchain? I've been told for years that these transactions are censorship resistant. I'm interested to hear about how we go about this.

PEARSON : This is a common misconception. Many would-be terrorists or money-laundering operations believed this until they started plotting to harm the United States or one of our allies. We've frozen billions in funds indefinitely. And when I say "allies" I'm speaking of not just our traditional allies like, say, France. Plotting a terrorist attack against China is also going to cause you to be holding a worthless bag of coins. We maintain a blacklist, and we share this with other intelligence agencies, as a mutual favor, when it comes to terrorist threats. The first thing to understand is that traditional blockchains require a huge open ledger, so we can see the path of transactions along a chain. We don't necessarily know who holds each account, but knowing which address holds the funds is easy.

Once an address gets blacklisted, the miners who operate at the federal government level stop processing the transactions. Most of the time, I should say, this is the case, but there are more sophisticated blockchains and sidechains that do allow some amount of anonymity, but these require heavier protocols, and even so aren't completely immune to all attacks.

REESE : So the United States has mining operations?

PEARSON : Certainly, it would be foolish not to. Not even a tenth of a percent of the Pentagon's budget is dedicated to mining operations, and this turns a small profit. Same for most other countries, most notably China. But in China all miners work closely with the government at all times and need approval by the government. In the US, private miners are, by and large, ideologically opposed to censorship, but at the same time, practically motivated and simply don't want to waste efforts mining a block that won't be part of the larger chain. By now it is well understood that if we are not processing transactions with certain address, the blocks containing these transactions are likely to become invalidated.

REESE : OK but doesn't this require that you have 51% of the mining operations?

PEARSON : Good question. The answer is no. You only need a positive amount to tip the balance slightly. If there is a 2% chance that a block will be orphaned because a miner includes a transaction, it's not rational to include that transaction. Once miners start applying this reasoning there's a cascading effect. Perhaps you've had this explained, but just in case: In most blockchains, the blocks are mined sequentially, each miner gets paid to mine a block, but if subsequent miners refuse to mine a block, they can go to the block that was created immediately prior to the block they would like to censor, and start from there and create what's called a fork. Then the offending block gets orphaned and is no longer part of the main chain. If the censored fork is shorter than the altered fork, it no longer is considered valid. So a miner loses their efforts by trying to continue mining on a chain that will eventually lose out. So you don't want to go astray and mine a block that's going to be orphaned, it's not rational.

Miners are rational. They also follows laws where required.

Recently, many miners are utilizing mining efficiency software, software that is designed to prioritize transactions. We have active contributers to the algorithms in most open source cryptocurrency ecosystems. We work in explicit cooperation with other intelligence agencies throughout the globe and use knowledge of the mining software to nudge miners to deprioritize transactions. Once they get deprioritized widely enough, they get dropped from the mempool. We've locked up billions in funds of terrorists using this method. This became standard practice almost a decade ago. There was a string of attacks in China, and Islamic Jihadists claimed responsibility. Chinese officials determined that much of the activity of this particular cell was financed by hackers who used ransomware and digital currencies. Ransomware Funded Terrorism, commonly abbreviated RFT, was obviously a menace that we would have to work globally to combat. The US and China were the largest victims and are of the same mind about combating this sort of terrorism. When this group began, this group filtered all of their payments through a few main addresses. China announced, loudly and clearly that it was demanding all miners stop mining transactions from these addresses. Any Chinese miner who mined such transactions would lose their license to mine. The United States has several departments that maintain mining operations. Out of solidarity and in an act of goodwill towards our Chinese counterparts in the fight against RFT, all United States government-run mining operations ceased mining these transaction. Technically, the edict was they weren't allowed to mine these transactions until they were eight blocks deep, at least in the case of Bitcoin. Private miners around the US followed by adding a patch that mimicked US official mining operations. This was simple economic principles in action. Each miner makes the choice whether they are going to mine these transactions or not, and the game theory says there's one Nash equilibrium: Nobody mines the transactions.

This effort was successful in tying up the funds. Ultimately, the terrorists who had attacked China had to pay huge transaction fees in order to push these transactions through, but this ended up costing the terrorists a huge portion of their coin. Of course, we knew where they sent the money, so we added these addresses to the list. We were dealing with smart people, so inevitably they stopped using the same few addresses and instead generated hundreds. So it took some effort for us, working with the Chinese, and Israel, to maintain a list of RFT addresses. The list mushroomed to thousands of addresses very quickly. Because the list was updated so dynamically, miners began using their own predictive tools to prioritize transactions so that they wouldn't end up mining a transaction that may be orphaned a block or two down the road. This created an unintended (but nevertheless welcome) decentralized censorship - if the machine learning algorithms detected that you were behaving in a way that would get your account flagged for RFT associations, the miners would just leave your transactions alone. With our beforehand knowledge of which addresses would be banned we were able to train the algorithm. Before adding to the banned list we would send the suspect accounts a certain amount of dust from certain agency accounts. Then shortly after, we add these accounts to the RFT list. The machine learning algorithms picked up on this. In the US there still is some significant amount of red-tape in adding an address to the censorship list, if we cross our T's and dot our I's, which we do, as this does amount to censorship. If we suspected an address of wrongdoing and wanted to freeze the account, a few dust transaction would signal to the crowd that we were thinking of censoring these transactions. We aren't censoring anybody at this point, just hinting to the community that we are thinking of censoring some addresses. The resulting effect is that the transactions are de facto censored. We use this tool quite frequently.

REESE : So you can get the crowd to perform censorship for you? What if you mis-identify a terrorist, is there any way to rectify this?

PEARSON : Yes, we have a whitelist. On multiple occasions, accounts were suspected of RFT and were later cleared. We explicitly added them to the whitelist. In fact, we created a fund to pay miners who mine recently white-listed transactions. To be fair, we don't agree with every decision of every other government regarding which transactions to censor or not to censor. For example, there exist a number of dissidents who disagree with their respective governments' ideologies, but in our estimation don't pose any sort of terrorist threat. We aggressively participate and encourage processing transactions involving these accounts. This counterbalances efforts by other governments that are not necessarily our allies.

REESE : You work with allies, or at least those with common interests to combat RFT. What about operations against global adversaries or hostile governments?

PEARSON : We employ a number of tactics. If there is a situation when one nation or coalition prefers and uses a digital currency, we can disrupt and deflate or inflate and facilitate, depending on whether it's a friend or foe. For example, during the recent civil war in Mali - the government was supported by corrupt Islamic extremists, and the rebellion was sympathetic to democratic and western values. The nation had issued a currency on the Alice blockchain. The rebels began using a colored coin version of this. We didn't want to attack the Alice blockchain itself, but we were able to artificially create demand for these colored coins. We did this by simply buying up the colored coins with our war chest. There's a significant multiplier effect in the price - and there's also a FOMO effect that induces global investors into the market. So the bank accounts of the opposition forces grew by orders of magnitude overnight. Next, we generated FUD propaganda which suggested that the colored coins were the only coins that would retain value, in particular, promoting the idea that the other coins issued by the government in power would end up being essentially worthless. This raised the buying power of the opposition, and decimated the economic power of the loyalists. This difference ultimately led to a decisive advantage.

It's extremely important that we do whatever we can to facilitate authority in these countries that is willing to create a healthy prosperity for their people, and this usually goes hand-in-hand with democratic values. This is consistent with US doctrines going back well into the last century.

REESE : What about human rights violations?

PEARSON : We've been working to deal with some of the more egregious acts of human trafficking and hostage-taking, in particular we focus on those involving digital currencies. We are mostly concerned with particularities of domestic security, but we do become involved when US citizens are targeted for extortion. Perhaps you are aware of the recent rash of ransom attempts: Kidnappers will kidnap a victim, hold them hostage at gun point, and then initiate a video conference. The attackers choose a somewhat wealthy but otherwise random Tapboard user in a more prosperous country and give them nine minutes to send $300 or they perform various acts on the person being kidnapped. This usually gives the person enough time to do a quick web search and discover that yes, they do follow through, this is real. This is horrifying. We are working will allies to bring law and order to the nations from whence this sort of extortion originates.

REESE : I'd like to ask about something that I heard in the course of these hearings. Paul Preston suggested that Department of Defense was instrumental in the attack on the Bitcoin blockchain.

PEARSON : I can confirm that DHS was involved. I probably won't give you as many details as you would like, as such may be risking sources and methods. However, I was briefed on Preston's testimony and can confirm that I indeed did meet with Preston, albeit as an officer of DHS. He is essentially correct in our objective. A North Korea emboldened with hundreds of billions of dollars of digital currency poses a threat - both a physical one and an economic one. Minimizing this threat falls directly under our purview.

REESE : Did you coordinate any military efforts as part of that campaign?

PEARSON : I'm not going to confirm or deny military operations other than I can confirm that we did coordinate this campaign with several other departments.

REESE : Who initiated this?

PEARSON : Officer Jay was alerted to this by Da. Da identified the objectives and asked us if we were interested. We responded that we would be interested. Soon after, Da invited us to participate in the planning. Zara was the liaison for that communication. We went by "Chandler" and we were supposed to play the role of a "disinterested but greedy whale, with knack for creating master trading scripts with AI." Da told us he set this up so that we could stay in the loop. Luckily for us, Zara does have an extensive background in machine learning, so she fit the role well.

REESE : Chandler was described to us as a "whale". Did you engage in trading activities that would be characterized as whale-like?

PEARSON : Not in this instance. Someone else was moving the market. Zara helped out with the AI but we didn't supply any of the funds or make the trades.

REESE : Do you have any intelligence to suggest this market-mover could have been Jing?

PEARSON : We have conflicting intelligence and opinions on this. We don't actually know if Jing is a single person or a group. He exhibits distinct multi-modal behaviors.

REESE : What do you mean by this?

PEARSON : We maintain a large data repository on every major player in the digital finance arena. There are a number of natural language processing statistics that can be applied - and Jing is funny in that his, or their, English is clustered into several statistical nodes. As if there was 6 or 7 people running the account. The most obvious explanation for this is that Jing doesn't speak English, and had a set of different translators.

REESE : Do you have any evidence that Jing is a single real person?

PEARSON : Direct evidence? We do not have such.

REESE : Now you've said that you were part of an operation that caused Bitcoin to crash in price - did this pose any sort of significant threat to our economy here in the US?

PEARSON : We did indeed consider this, and commissioned a classified report assessing this. In short we determined that as Bitcoin was largely a speculative investment - meaning that, there isn't much of the economy built on Bitcoin itself, at least built such that a price crash would damage the business beyond speculators losing investments. So while a price crash posed a financial risk to a few individual players, we felt that the benefits of decimating North Korea's war chest far outweighed a very small minority of investors' nest eggs.

REESE : In regards to this group of people who crashed Bitcoin, would you describe these people as politically motivated, or just financially motivated?

PEARSON : Everything we observed indicated a financial motivation.

REESE : So there was no hostility toward the US or democracy?

PEARSON : If there was hostility, perhaps they were smart enough to hide this hostility from Homeland Security agents.

REESE : Do you monitor the heavy-hitters in the international cryptocurrency scene?

PEARSON : Absolutely.

REESE : Are you aware of any person or group who is hostile towards the United States or to democratic values?

PEARSON : At lower levels, of course, you always have quite a vast number of individuals hostile to our interests. Among the "heavy hitters," though, some of the wealthiest individuals are US citizens, and while politically they tend to lean towards libertarianism, they aren't considered hostile to the US.

REESE : Who is the wealthiest?

PEARSON : We believe, of course, it's impossible to attribute every dollar to every party, but we believe that Jing is the wealthiest holder of digital financial instruments.

REESE : What exactly do we know about Jing?

PEARSON : Actually, Officer Jay is sort of an expert on Jing. I think your questions are best answered by Zara. She has interacted with Jing directly and covertly for some time.

REESE : Are you personally familiar with Jing? When did you first interact with Jing?

JAY : I've been acquainted with Jing for quite some time, going back to when he initially invested in Tapboard. I guess I should preface this with the caveat that I've never met Jing in any sort of physical capacity but was introduced via email by James Andrews. I can talk through that if you like?

REESE : Please.

JAY : I'll start from the beginning. I was brought into the fold at Tapboard fairly early. I wasn't considered a founder, as the founders were Scott who you all know and love and another fellow named James. James and I had a peculiar relationship, suffice to say. James was unceasingly impressed with everything I was doing, and was constantly picking my brain, mining for nuggets of understanding in various aspects of algorithms and consensus mechanisms. We spent copious amounts of time discussing mathematics. James was determined to understand Derived Categories. At some point James began fussing excessively about Scott, in really, sort of alarming and inappropriate ways. I made a good effort to ignore this, and started to create distance between myself and James, not having required the services of a vulgar racist at that time in my life. To give you a flavor, James was repeatedly amused by his own suggestion that Scott return to his job at Global Pharmacy selling Viagra in a cubicle in India. Now while I thought Scott could be a little bit uptight and lack in humor - he is insanely uptight by the way - it was a running challenge to see who could entice him into using marijuana - but everyone knew he was very good at what he did. Trying to apply this stereotype always seemed a little puerile to me. James would also pontificate on his theories that Scott was some sort of megalomaniac narcissist who wanted no less than world domination. I still went by David at the time, but was beginning my transition, and didn't really have time in my life for toxic characters who were so flamboyantly insecure. But James was the other founder and the majority stakeholder, and so I did find myself interacting with him, even as he seemed to come unraveled. The day I affirmed myself to the team as Sara, James began losing screws at an accelerating rate. He acted strangely, asking a number of strange, exceeding inappropriate questions. I was furious and I didn't speak to him for several weeks after that, and politely told him I wanted nothing to do with him. Scott was cordial, as he usual is, but he didn't seem to care about how James was treating me, that was strictly between James and I, he insisted. At some point a bit later James sends me a message and says that he has been having, what he describes as a "slow motion mental breakdown" - he tells me that he's coming apart, that he wants to sell his stake, that he want to move somewhere and find peace - on an island or somewhere. He wanted to offer his Tapboard stake to me first, at a discount, but he also wanted to know if I had connections with anybody who wanted to buy his stake - he wanted this to be a one-time negotiated over-the-counter transaction. This struck me to be his weird tortured way of apologizing, as he knew I couldn't come up with upwards of several hundred million dollars to buy his share. It was actually sort of sweet, in a pathetic way. I tried to meet him were he was at, and took this as sincere. Now I didn't know anybody of the sort, and it did not seem in his best interest for me to post messages with this information around like this, so I told him I would keep my eyes and ears open. Shortly after, perhaps the next day, James posts a message, publicly, saying that he had found a buyer for 2/3 of his stake, a Chinese fellow named Jing, and he was also about to close with someone else for the other 1/3. I had never heard Jing's name, and James had never mentioned to me any dealings with Chinese crypto kingpins. I did scope around the message boards and he seemed to have a reputation for being in the know, and anticipating government actions somehow. I suppose he may have approached James. James sent a very flattering message to Jing introducing me and explaining that I was the best developer and marketing strategist Tapboard would ever have. I never spoke to James again, I hope he found a nice archipelago and some repose. But James had been the majority shareholder - he sold a majority share to Jing, which made Jing the largest, but not a majority stakeholder.

REESE : How would you characterize Jing's role in Tapboard at this time?

JAY : As I said, a significant stake, but less than majority stake in Tapboard was held by Jing. I didn't have any expectation for what Jing expected of me, as I wasn't privy to the conversations between James and Jing. I was essentially an acting vice president of research and Scott was CEO, and now we had this other major stakeholder, as James had dropped out of the picture. Jing never reached out directly to me, or to Scott, as far I know. But Jing was never shy to communicate. Always on public channels or Tapboards. Jing made it clear very soon that he was to be a classic activist stakeholder. There were a number of fairly minor governance proposals for upgrades to the consensus software, and Jing voted all of his stake in every one of these, even the most minor ones. And he would post extensive public questions in various Tapboards, wanting the cost benefit analysis for each proposal. He knew quite well the details of what was going on, more so than you would expect for an investor. So Jing was definitely what you would call an active investor. At the time, we were essentially a messaging app with a hybrid blockchain, in theory decentralized, but in practice heavily centralized. Our governance, however, was decentralized and permissionless. Jing wanted to build a bit more blockchain infrastructure, beyond just payments and social media - and dive into all of the heavy industrial undertaking like supply chains. Jing apparently owned a stake in several other governance protocols, including a significant stake in the dominant decentralized exchange protocols. So he proposed a merger - a "preferred layering," really, which ended up being quite beneficial to all parties. We didn't have the infrastructure at the time, to say, write smart contracts to track coffee as the product travels its way from Ethiopia to the US, while executing futures and delivery contracts, but other protocols did. So essentially we ended up paying out for developers to forge this connection, and this was all Jing's idea. It worked well. It also paid off quite handsomely for Jing, as the network effect kicked in and the value of his assets all around appreciated quite handsomely. But he went beyond that, threatening to pull support for proposals that he didn't like, and taking unexpected political stances. This became somewhat of an obstacle. We were working for global market share at the time, in particular in underdeveloped nations and there was some fierce competition with EWD. Jing announced we wouldn't be working with Ghana, because they were corrupt, so said Jing. This was quite an unusual statement coming from a blockchain activist trader in China - the operating assumption held by armchair blockchain ethicists is that much of the world is at least somewhat corrupt but that the best we can do is to bring prosperity to as much of the world as possible and hope that with it comes some progress on these fronts. Singling out Ghana was a strange choice. About this time, another Chinese national, a guy named Da, emerged as the other holder who had purchased James' stake. Da was also new and unfamiliar to me. Da claimed to be 16 years old, and Jing had some insatiable spite for him. I don't know what their relationship was back in China, but Jing was furious at James for allowing Da a stake, claiming it was a travesty, totally inappropriate for Jing to be unequally yoked with such a low-class uneducated peasant like Da. Da was idealistic and full of energy, and the public spats between Da and Jing were often epic and entertaining when they weren't extremely frightening. Da wrote a beautiful piece in defense of Ghana, and even accused Jing of perpetuating corruption in China. The community was alarmed, perceiving this as a shots-fired statement, but somehow this particular conflict sublimated into the atmosphere and the two of them continued to persist in a healthy balance. Eventually, we did end up working significantly with the government in Ghana, and Jing publicly apologized.

REESE : So this feud between Da and Jing. How did this conflict display itself?

JAY : There are a number of stories. I'll begin with XXY example, which is perhaps the most illustrative.

About a year or so in, there was a major governance question on how certain supply-chain contracts were to be executed. As always, we were constantly onboarding more functionality, offering more interoperability. Tapcoin runs on a layered protocol, which uses the decentralized exchange for parts of the settlement and our native Tapcoin as counterpart. We had merged with Ricci, after some competition, and now we were attempting to construct a dominating global network, capable of executing every type of settlement contract you could dream of. We had a major decision as to how the layer was supposed to be structured. The technicalities are exceeding boring, but please bear with me just a little bit. At issue here was whether the embedded futures contract could be granted direct access to certain escrow accounts on an external blockchain. The alternative was to create mirrored layers. At first this seems like an engineering and design problem, but the ramifications were potentially financially significant. Very significant. For both of the options there were external parties who had solutions, or claimed to have solutions that were somewhat ready-to-go, but would take a bit of time to implement and each would incur overhead and small costs going forward. There were liability concerns from a regulatory perspective, and these were unfolding with considerable uncertainty. There were credible arguments from legal counsel on both sides of the issue that the other protocol could cause problems in certain jurisdictions. Depending on how regulatory agencies chose to classify these mirrored layers could make or break the protocol. If you think this is boring so far, and your sleeping eyes speak volumes to this, Senator Reese, I won't even bother discussing the meetings were I heard the words "fiduciary obligations" thrown around for 8 hours a day for two weeks.

Anyways, it so happened that the two external protocols being considered were called XXX and XXZ. The decision was somewhat fraught, as no matter how it was done, we would be picking favorites. Plan A would favor XXX, which was by now an established and generally well-regarded blockchain protocol, while plan B would favor XXZ, an emerging and promising protocol. At the scale we were aiming for, the decision would necessarily make a difference in the range of hundreds of millions of dollars per year. So naturally, there's a lot of lobbying going on, leading up to the vote. Supporters of Plan A were constantly expounding upon the virtues of their protocol tweak, while Plan B's proponents were calling Plan A a recipe for disaster and so forth. Almost predictably, Da and Jing chose to back different horses. Jing was stridently one-sided in favor of

XXX and joined the Plan A team. I assumed at the time that he had an undisclosed stake and was in position to profit from Plan A, and I also assumed Da was just being contrarian by backing Plan B. But I wasn't sure. The stakeholders in the competing protocols presumable had non-trivial stakes in our protocol. So there was a significant amount of wealth and value at play.

Now we have a way to settle disputes. We had inherited in our recent partnership with Ricci a voting protocol that was a variant of ranked choice. Closer to STAR (Score, Then Automatic Runoff) voting, but even more expressive. Voting methods on a blockchain where the basic assumption is some amount of sophistication can veer into some exceeding wonky territory, as I'm sure you can imagine.

The voting protocol is a single election, with an automatic runoff between the top two proposals. In essence, stakeholders score the proposals relative to each other, and then the runoff is simply a classic head to head - determined by the weighted count of voters that preferred one over the other. It was believed that there was minimal incentive to vote dishonestly, and the Condorcet winner was supposed to win whenever at least 50% voted honestly. Because it was an automated runoff, you wanted to get your proposal to the final round and then hope your proposal compares favorably to the competitor. Again, Da is pushing Plan B, Jing is backing Plan A. They publicly debated each other on the merits of each. It seemed that Da was gaining traction, his proposal seemed to be more popular among Tapcoin and Alice users and seemed to be on track to win. Da was slightly more popular and this made up for the smaller portion of stake that he held personally. But it was tight, coming down to the decision block.

With about one week before the final vote, a third proposal shows up unexpectedly. (Actually there were dozens of others, most of these were garbage - it costs about $2.90 to submit one.) This proposal called itself XXY and claimed that it combined the best features of both protocols. It was backed by a unknown but apparently well-educated team out of Singapore. This XXY proposal was vetted and it seemed to make sense, except for one thing, there was significant cost, both upfront and continuing.

Not to bore you to death, but our ten-year partnership with Ricci involved the creation of an additional treasury fund devoted to Tapcoin related infrastructure investments. Essentially this is just fresh Alice, minted and distributed. You could call this a slush fund. This new proposal required that 75% of this fund was transfered to the XXY blockchain and minted at a rate higher than we had originally intended. Further, the ongoing transaction fee would be somewhat noticeable: While Plans A and B both seemed to add about 1-1.5% costs to the overhead, this XXY would add 5-7%. This was a non-starter amongst almost everybody. Most holders of Alice didn't really care so much about supply-chain issues, but they were uncomfortable with the devaluing of the coin upfront. The users who concerned themselves with supply chain issues didn't want to shell out this high of a fee, as this cut into the competitive advantage of the whole platform, to the point where it may have been only narrowly profitable, if at all. Suffice to say, it did not appear that XXY was a proposal to be contended with seriously. When it showed up on the proposals list it seemed no more than a "hail Mary" attempt from an emergent team from Singapore. For the vote, neither Jing nor Da controlled enough of the voting to be decisive. Both needed support from stakeholders who were essentially swing voters. Jing had a keen understanding of the voting method used in Ricci and pointed out, in an ostensibly off-the-cuff cavalier post, that by burying Plan B in the scoring related to this alternative XXY, it was possible, with a somewhat concerted effort, Plan B would end up below XXY and not proceed to the automatic runoff. This is classic strategic voting, exploiting the rules of the voting system. Rationally, nearly everybody preferred to not have the XXY, so in the runoff, if Da was relegated to third place, it would appear to be an easy slam-dunk runoff win for Jing. It wasn't clear how serious Jing was at the time, but some of his cheerleading fanbase quickly became atingle with the idea, and began evangelizing this rabidly, computing exactly how to strategically vote in order to bury Da's proposal. Again, the goal was to doom Da and Plan B to third place, leaving Jing and Plan A in a runoff with XXY. Da responded in turn, directly telling his crowd that Jing was attempting to bury their proposal, countering with his own method to bury Jing's proposal. According to Da's published analysis, it was more likely that the XXY proposal would defeat Jing and the runoff would be between Da and XXY. If Jing had been joking at first, he was locked in now.

In blockchain elections, you are allowed to vote early in the sense that you can submit signed voting transactions to the mempool in advance. These aren't processed until the election blocks, but you can submit them. You may also submit a contradictory vote. If you have two contradictory votes, the miners are free to choose which vote ends up on the chain. Now Jing did this, submitted his votes, several days ahead - voting his stake in a way that buried Plan B below all and put XXY just below Plan A. Da followed suit. Now Jing then announced that he had less to lose, because Da was more popular, and so he said, now somewhat famously "we welcome the chicken game." Da responds, "yes, we welcome the chicken game because exactly as you say, our proposal is more popular." It was still possible as the selection block approached that either could also submit a competing vote, at this point the miners could, in theory, make a decisive choice which votes to include, provided the valid votes existed. We all expected this would happen and it would be up to the miners to decide. But neither Jing nor Da yielded. Neither signed other transactions. The election arrived and Da's followerbase had indeed given Jing's proposal the lowest possible score, dooming Jing's Plan A to third place. Jing's people had done the exact same thing and it was very close - the runoff was indeed between Da and XXY. However, there was a wrinkle: apparently 10% of the votes cast chose XXY over both Da and Jing. With all of Jing's voters choosing Da below XXY, the XXY proposal ended up winning the runoff. We were startled, and didn't know how to proceed - this was not supposed to happen, and led to a bit of a constitutional crisis of consensus. Immediately you had people suggesting a hard fork, but the trouble was that Da and Jing were inexorably at loggerheads, thus a hard fork threatened to destroy the entire chain. Our best option was to accept the results of the election with resignation and move forward. Da and Jing would need to live with the results of their inflexibility. Ultimately, the XXY proposal was not the consummate disaster we had feared. Indeed it was somewhat cost inefficient, the overhead for each transaction being paid to this XXY was about 4.8% - not quite as bad as the initial projections but our industry typically shoots for under 1%. Obviously this was not the best outcome, however it did not destroy us completely. We hoped that Da and Jing would come away wiser from the incident - perhaps choosing to avoid this "chicken game" when it comes to governance voting.

REESE : Interesting. Do we know much about the folks in position to profit from the XXY proposal?

JAY : About a week later someone claiming to be a major stakeholder from XXY announced that playing Da and Jing against each other had been their objective the entire time. We thought this person who posted this was a troll at first, due to the braggadocious locution of the post, but he or she did hold a majority stake in XXY - I verified this - and they also posted a generous amount of purportedly personal information about Jing and Da, trolling and mocking them. This person also remained anonymous but identified themselves as the CEO of the company that had submitted the proposal.

REESE : As you may know, we seem to have very little information on either Da or Jing. This third party claimed to have inside information on these two. Did you verify any of it?

JAY : We didn't have an indisputable method for doing this. Not that you should read much from this, but they both contested vehemently that this third party knew them at all. None of the described assertions fall into the category of things I put faith in.

REESE : Do you know who this third person is?

JAY : I came up with a speculative guess, but with very little hard evidence.

REESE : Who would this be?

JAY : Actually, Scott Greywahl. Now. I - I should go back. I should be measured and cautious with my words here.

I had begun to wonder if James was not so crazy after all. As I've alluded to before, James told me not infrequently that Scott had diabolical plans, that Scott would lie and cheat, that Scott was somehow inhuman, had no soul, no empathy, and was always looking for ways to collect rent eternally. James had essentially predicted something like this. I tried to contact James but was unable to, as he seemed to have fallen off the planet, true to his word. Don't get me wrong, I do think James was more than a little crazy, but may have been spot-on regarding Scott. It makes perfect sense. I knew that James was crazy, everybody knew James was crazy, so who am I going to trust? I began looking into this a little bit deeper, not under the guise of suspicion of Scott, instead as a general cyber-forensic peaking around. The thing I didn't understand was that Scott was most definitely not, at least according to anybody who appeared to have knowledge of this sort of thing, involved with Chinese politics in any way. Scott was born and raised in New Jersey. So I wasn't convinced. But this became very fascinating for me, trying to unearth who this person was. I wanted it to not be Scott.

REESE : Did something end up convincing you?

JAY : There was one particular moment that stands out. About three weeks after the incident, Scott called me in and asked me directly if I knew who this third party was. I began enumerating the myriad leads and he stopped me short and just said that it would be best if I just dropped it - whoever this was hadn't done anything illegal. After all, the game was the game and this was how it was played. Further, XXY would make great partners anyways and everything would be fine and we should just move forward. When Scott said this, the movie reel in my mind began projecting all the previous interactions with Scott and I suddenly was struck by the overwhelming feeling that Scott was behind this, along with unpleasant taste that was curiously reminiscent of my lower intestines. This seemed so selfish, so perverted and sociopathic. If the narrative I had constructed in my head to this point was true, this guy had played (and quite skillfully I might add) Jing and Da against each other so that he could add a not insignificant amount of income to his already immense wealth and was now casually and coldly telling me not to worry about it.

I could not believe that I hadn't seen it before: Once you see that someone is a sociopath, your eyes are open, and you are indelibly unable to unsee the sociopathic behavior. Every move they make suddenly makes sense as that of a sociopath. James had told me stories. These stories required a struggle to believe, and so I didn't believe them. James tried to explain to me while I laughed him off - sociopaths do things so unfathomably horrible so that if the victims do describe these horrible things to other people, other people will inevitably come to the simplest conclusion: that the victims are just crazy. Again, it makes sense - I thought James was crazy at the time, so I didn't believe him. But sociopaths count on this dynamic.

At the time Tapboard was surging forward in several directions. We had already led with a dominant messaging platform, and had recently established ourselves in blockchain tech, including the supply chain technology we had recently onboarded. We had our foot in the door as far as e-commerce, and our next goal was to move fully into social media content so to begin generating our own advertising revenue. Scott was very excited about this, and created a new division of the company for me: Social Media Research. He invited me into his office to present this to me, and explained that the key to advertising was conflict: The best way to deliver consumers to advertisers was to bring out the worst partisanship. Partisanship weakens customers and makes them more amenable to advertisers suggestions. Partisan engagement also gives you more expressive metrics on the customers themselves. Not his exact words, but in essence, that's what he wanted me to create. I was to lead the AI team in charge of user timelines - Scott told me that the design of the algorithms should aim to maximize partisan engagement. That's when I decided to quit. I told Scott at that time that I was done - I had joined Tapboard, when Tapboard was nascent, a fun new encrypted messaging app, and now it had become just another Facebook, but for people under 60, and in fact something even more beastly. I didn't say anything about the XXY debacle, but it was on my mind. I left his office and haven't spoken to him since.

REESE : And has he contacted you?

JAY : About a week later, I received a message signed from the address claiming to be behind the XXY manipulation, saying that, in more words or less, that I should just keep my mouth shut about things that would get me and my family into trouble. The day after that I submitted an application to Homeland Security cyberterrorism division. I find the role of cyber sleuth preferable to the role of cyber manipulator.

REESE : OK. I'm going to ask you a question, please think carefully about how you want to answer it. You don't have to answer it, but it may help us get to know what's going on. OK? You've been saying some very damning things about Mr. Greywahl. Do you think Mr. Greywahl could have orchestrated the attack on the election?

JAY : Scott is priapically greedy and his behavior is consistent with descriptions of a sociopath, but all this, this seems to stretch a bit beyond his wheelhouse. I have stepped away from Scott and gained perspective over the last 4 years. I was never able to tie him definitively to the manipulations with XXY. On the other hand, it has the markings of something he might be behind - exploiting conflict for profit. However, I do not see the profit motive. In honesty, Tapboard is malware. Their bread and butter is to collect your financial proclivities, by tracking your every move and deliver these nicely curated packages of human behavior to the corporations most poised to exploit it. Profit motivates Scott. In regards to the current situation, I do not see exactly the means or methods of profit, except for to raise the profile of Tapboard. But frankly, I do not comprehend the reasoning: Tapboard has saturated the market, so inviting regulations and scrutiny endangers more than it assists. I do know that Scott likes to calculate. I think that disrupting the elections do not make sense from any rational perspective. I'm going to guess 'no.'

REESE : Now speaking of Da, is Da dead?

JAY : The cluster of accounts we've associated to Da appear to be dormant. Which is consistent with Da's demise.

REESE : To your knowledge, has anyone met Da?

JAY : I haven't talked to anybody who has described him first person. I only look at the online fingerprints.

REESE : Do you think we would be able to get a hold of James? Did James ever meet Da?

JAY : I don't know if James met Da. Funny though, I received a message this morning from a new address. It said "I hate to be right, well not actually, I love being right. I hear you're going to visit the Senate. Go give 'em hell, Sara." I haven't replied, but I feel certain this is from James. He obviously has some knowledge of these hearings, whatever island he landed on.

REESE : So you're in communication with James? I can speak with the rest of the committee, but I for one would like to add James to the witness list if possible, as he seems to know all the players here personally.

JAY : You want me to message him back, I mean, I can do this right now, do you have to issue a subpoena or use some official channels?

REESE : If he's on "some island" as you say, we may not have much luck in compelling his testimony.

JAY : Seriously though, I could reply right now. I'm happy to, in fact. "James. Long time no see what up - hey - a certain Senate subcommittee would love to rap thanx lemme know." Send. Easier beg forgiveness than to be granted permission, so I'm told?

REESE : OK. Let us know if he gets in touch. I have no further questions.

CHAIR : We will have a brief meeting following this testimony regarding potential witness James Andrews. The chair recognizes the Ranking Member Silva.

SILVA : Thanks. I realize you can't discuss all sources and methods in this setting. But I'd like to ask some sort of general questions. First of all, it seems like, from your opening remarks, Ms. Pearson, that you use a variety of classic approaches to furthering US interests. Could one reasonably assume that hostile governments are using similar methods?

PEARSON : Yes, absolutely. In some regards, the tools have changed but the basic methods have not changed in the last century.

SILVA : If you were to try to sow confusion in another democratic election process, how would you do this?

PEARSON : Well, nations that strive to maintain legitimate democratic elections are allies of ours, pretty much across the board. We would have no desire to do this.

SILVA : OK, this is more of a hypothetical. What would you use?

PEARSON : This is classic PSYOP. I'd say the main tool in this day would be embedded personae. Spread cynicism. Spread fear, uncertainty and doubt.

SILVA : Can you tell me a little bit about these personae.

PEARSON : I believe I can without endangering sources. Of course we don't want to out any of these personae, but it should come as no surprise that we maintain hundreds of social media and developer profiles with the objective of exhibiting influence on cryptocurrency use throughout the world, as well as providing advanced intel on movements in the cryptocurrency markets. These are designed to mimic real-life cryptocurrency influencers and open source project contributors. Many of these have very strong development background and are active contributors on open source blockchain projects. Some of them claim to run or actually do run businesses in various parts of the world, many of them quite profitable. As far as developing agents, the cover story is easy, you know, so-and-so is an independently wealthy developer who made boatloads of money in the early days of Bitcoin and now lives in Ernest Hemingway's old apartment in Paris, or whatever, and contributes to open source projects, as a hobby. In the cryptocurrency community bizarre stories and people are more common than not. Nobody questions you if you have a little bit of domain knowledge.

SILVA : So you would believe that other nations also use such a technique?

PEARSON : Oh, absolutely.

SILVA : So do you think that either Da or Jing is a state-backed persona?

PEARSON : We always consider that a possibility unless we know otherwise. At this point we don't know otherwise.

SILVA : Is it normal that you would be unable to confirm or deny that crypto-currency heavy hitters are organic?

PEARSON : Necessarily, some of the people who have become billionaires have chosen to be reclusive in day-to-day life, often for obvious security reasons. It's not unusual. We are aware of high school math teachers, mailmen, even popular musicians who have made millions of dollars trading coins and have continued with their life and have told no one, but do maintain elaborate profiles online that are nothing like reality. It's almost like a form of cos-play. So if you say "organic" I'm not really sure what you mean. There's levels of fiction. Who you are online is who you are online.

SILVA : What is your opinion as to the objectives of those behind the election attacks?

PEARSON : This was a very well funded attack, which suggests a well-motivated adversary. Often, if you attack a nation without any specific, identifiable goals, the point is simply to make the nation look bad, and breed cynicism. Some global adversary who wants us to look bad? I don't have any more than speculation at this point.

SILVA : I want to return to the theory that has been put forth that this was somewhat of an inside job, organized by Scott Greywahl, in an attempt to drive future elections to blockchain technology. Is this something you see as feasible?

PEARSON : Zara?

JAY : Again, the possibility exists, but the motivation doesn't follow. It doesn't track for me that Scott would use his own system to attack the election so that the future elections would be held on Tapboard. I do believe that Scott has the resources to pull this off but the motivating theory does not seem credible in my opinion.

SILVA : OK. Whose job is it to make sure this doesn't happen?

PEARSON : While this precise scenario wasn't laid out in any manual we've been given, I would take responsibility for it. I regret that our agents and officers had been unable to identify this threat sooner.

SILVA : Can you point to specific failures?

PEARSON : By and large, our operation typically involves aggressively responding to very specific threats. Most of these threats are somewhat predictable, like terrorist organizations. What we've offered is new tools in attacking these known threats. We have an active watch on hundreds of organizations that we consider hostile to the US. What caught us flat-footed was that this particular attack did not come from sources that we had identified as hostile. It was a confluence of noisy operations, some older, darker money, and some very sophisticated tumbling technology that prevented us from seeing clearly that there was an attack under way until it was too late. The consensus had been up until election day that there was just an uptick of random election motivated odd behaviors.

But we dropped the ball. These things happen. I recall very well making a decision to pursue a career in intelligence nearly three decades ago when somehow 19 men evaded US intelligence and flew planes into buildings. There's always more to learn, there's always the unknown unknowns. So here we are now. We have a lot to learn. Our job is never done.

SILVA : And how will your operations change moving forward?

PEARSON : At this point, we're still very early in the investigation. Step 1 is a thorough investigation. With my PSYOP background I have to admit that I'm, for lack of a better word, impressed. Despite the size of this operation it had a very delicate touch. However, I will use this setting to issue a bit of a warning that lawmakers in your position should consider: There is a point at which the technology leaves us so exposed that it may be up to people in your positions to reign in certain types of PSYOP against America. Current global conditions are a hostile PSYOPs dream: billions of people connected to the internet, with massive amounts of information on everybody else for sale on both legal and illicit markets, billions of hungry workers throughout the globe who are willing to perform small tasks, misinformation abounding to the point were many people are experiencing "truth fatigue" and sophisticated AI technology that can predict human behavior quite well on a large scale. This is a problem that won't go away, and I'm afraid we won't be so good at the whack-a-mole game if this situation continues. We live in a global era, this is undeniable and we will do our best, but at the moment, US consumers of social media are sitting ducks.

SILVA : Anything else you think might be relevant about Jing or Da or any other names?

PEARSON : I should mention one sort of strange observation. We are pretty sure that Jing funded the Real People Project.

SILVA : This is the project where the names of average Joe's are put on the ballot?

PEARSON : Yes. No reason given, just this project pops up claiming they want to see real people on the ballot. We tracked the funds because it was such a ridiculously large amount, and we are pretty sure the source is Jing.

SILVA : What do you make of this?

PEARSON : Honestly, my professional assessment is not-a-damn clue. The names made it on the ballot, but there was no campaign, no follow-up. I don't see the endgame.

SILVA : Thank you for your time. I have no further questions.

7

TESTIMONY OF THE FIFTH WITNESS. Mr. Joshua Finney, West Springfield, VA.

CHAIR : Good morning. Shortly we are expecting video testimony from James Andrews. We are setting that up at the moment. We also have another new witness. Yesterday, our next witness, Joshua Finney approached the Fairfax County Sheriff and identified himself as possibly having pertinent information. Joshua Finney is a musician at Our Redeemer Lutheran Church and believes he provided the key that was used to plant the explosive device.

To begin, the chair recognizes Ranking Member Silva.

SILVA : We appreciate you identifying yourself to the Sheriff's Office and coming forward. Obviously you know this is very important.

FINNEY : Thanks, I'm sorry I was involved in this and I'm hoping I can help in any way possible.

SILVA : How long have you been with Our Redeemer Lutheran Church?

FINNEY : About 8 years.

SILVA : Why did you have a key?

FINNEY : I am involved with the worship band. We have a small church band that rehearses on Thursdays. I'm the director, more or less.

SILVA : How many other people have a key?

FINNEY : Probably two dozen? No idea really. The locks have not been changed that I can recall.

SILVA : So how were you approached? Lead us through this.

FINNEY : Early in the summer - already a bit back, I received a Tapboard message out of the blue - someone asked me if I had a key. I ignored this, because it was a totally weird request, but then two days later, I get another strange message saying that they represent a wealthy individual who is doing sort of a vanity project during the summer, and what they need is a key. I then received $2000, no strings attached. So I responded, why don't you just ask Pastor Nelson, and they said the project only works if the reverend doesn't realize what's going on. They described this again as some sort of spirituality research. They insisted it had to be double-blind, they couldn't let anyone at the church know what they were up to or the experiments wouldn't be valid. Then they said that although they do understand that approaching people and asking people to get the keys in exchange for a sum of money could come off as weird, the individual they represented had literally billions of dollars, they wouldn't miss $55,000 here or there, and this was a pet project of theirs. This number grabbed me - I was in debt $55,000 and I was about to default. A default would cost me my house and tons of problems down the road. So I said, y'know, $55,000 sounds great. I was immediately sent $25,500 and was told I get the other half after I placed the key under the trash can north of the church that night. So I made a copy and did this and sure enough, was given the additional $27,500. They thanked me and said it was more than likely I probably wouldn't even notice.

SILVA : Can you describe the person who contacted you?

FINNEY : It was a picture of a blond professional looking woman, about 30 years old. Her name was Amelia, I believe. It looked credible.

SILVA : Now you said you were $55,000 in debt? Is this a coincidence?

FINNEY : I don't see how it could be. I had signed one of these viscous electronic mortgage contracts and had signed up for a .5% reduction in mortgage rate provided they deduct automatically from a Tapcoin account that I keep filled, but the fine print, or I guess, the code that nobody reads, is that if you default, they have this rapidly escalating series of hoops you have to jump through that just execute automatically, just to make it right, and full default means they just get the title to your home. It's a smart contract so there's literally nothing you can do except for keep the Tapcoin account loaded, and there sure as heck isn't a customer service line. I had reduced my hours due to a family medical emergency and failed to make payments, and one thing led to another, and I was about one week without $55,000 of losing my home to a smart contract.

SILVA : What was your job?

FINNEY : I run a local TapInstant distribution center. Technically, I'm a small business, but everything I do is as a contractor for Tapboard. They chose the house for me so that I would be strategically located and set me up with the mortgage lender. You know when you want toothpaste at 10:00 pm? That's me, at your door with the toothpaste at 10:05. It turns out it's a lot of work and the pay may or may not be minimum wage after all is said and done. So when my oldest child got sick, I found myself losing money quickly. You have to take yourself offline for certain amounts of time, and there's penalties for this. I never expected financial difficulties, so I never read the fine print or tried to understand how the contract works. But I found myself in a situation where if I didn't come up with money I would be out on the street with a sick child.

SILVA : Wow. Have you had a lawyer look through this contract?

FINNEY : A lawyer? I was working every hour I could and taking care of my sick son the rest of the time. I had neither the money nor the time to seek out a lawyer and try to explain this whole thing. Blockchain lawyers charge like $2000 for a consultation from what I hear. So yeah, once I was offered $55,000 I took it. I don't know how they knew, but I'm pretty sure they knew that this was my magic number.

SILVA : So did you ever have any other contact with this Amelia or anyone else?

FINNEY : None. Just a brief series of Tapboard DMs and then I left the key where they said.

SILVA : Did this request strike you as odd?

FINNEY : Obviously, yes, but it had enough credibility, looking back, it had enough credibility that you can believe it for $55,000. These debt contracts are nasty. I know many people who have lost homes unfairly due to the fine print in these smart contracts. I couldn't afford, literally, to mess it up.

SILVA : Had you indicated to anyone, on the internet or in the community, that you were in debt?

FINNEY : Certainly not on the internet. Close family were sort of aware that we were struggling, but I never mentioned, you know, a number. I was somewhat sensitive and self-conscious about my debt issues. It wasn't something I wore on my sleeve. To be honest I was ashamed I had been suckered into this contract.

SILVA : Is it possible this information was available via inspecting the smart contract?

FINNEY : My understanding is that if someone knew specifics of my address, and could do some reverse engineering, then yes, they may be able to observe an outstanding debt.

SILVA : Did you use your account in any way that could have been associated with the church's public address?

FINNEY : Actually, yes, when I was more gainfully employed I would use this account to give to the church. Also, more recently, I had used the church's account to reimburse some musical equipment. So we had transactions both ways.

SILVA : Is there anything else you'd like to tell us?

FINNEY : I'd just like to reiterate that I'm sorry I was involved in this.

SILVA : I have no further questions.

8

TESTIMONY OF THE SIXTH WITNESS. Mr. James Andrews.

CHAIR : Good Morning, Mr.Andrews. Thank you for agreeing to attend this video conference. This is a meeting of a select Senate Intelligence sub-committee created to study the attacks on the recent election. We've been conducting interviews this week attempting to get an understanding of the events leading to the postponement of the midterm elections. Your name has been mentioned by multiple witnesses as someone who may know a little bit more about certain individuals whose names have been arising in the testimony. So again, thanks for joining us. The full committee is in attendance, but the procedure is that we are going to allow Ranking Member Silva to ask you questions first, followed by Senator Reese.

ANDREWS : Good Morning to you, Senator. I'm looking forward to this opportunity.

SILVA : Good Morning, Mr. Andrews. Perhaps you could start by giving the committee a little background on yourself and your relation to the cryptocurrency industry.

ANDREWS : Certainly. My name is James Andrews. Please call me James. I'm 30 years old. I went to high school in Alexandria, and then went to a liberal arts college where I spent the first year and a half getting indoctrinated by the social justice hogwash brigade. About halfway through my sophomore year, the world was stricken by a giant collective delusion that a mundane flu virus was some sort of Armageddon, so my sophomore year finished with me in my mother's basement day-trading the stock market. I made almost a quarter of million dollars that spring and summer day-trading, and decided that obviously, I didn't need to go back to learn about how to ethically spend my not-really-exactly-hard-earned money without hurting anybody's feelings. After the stock market settled down I moved into trading crypto full time. I fell in with a group of people online, most notably, Scott, and later also David, and we formed an unofficial trading group. We were really interested in making money off novel boutique-ish tokens, but because there's a lot of lobbying and other annoying regulatory and other work to get these listed on the big exchanges, we did everything we could to push mainstreaming decentralized exchanges. We built Tapboard as a decentralized messaging app with decentralized asset trading capabilities. Scott is a real whiz as far as programming, and I had several million dollars in capital to get us started. So we split it 80-20 at first. It was a bit slow, so we figured out a way to partially centralize it - it turns out most people are willing to pay a few dollars a year to delegate hosts. That's how it got it's structure - it was originally intended to be fully decentralized, but that wasn't satisfying for most users, and a bit slow, instead you can just join in to your local or other preferred server for a small fee. The fact that you had choice made a big difference and pretty soon, as you all know, people where doing this even if they weren't into crypto or trading or gaming. So this started to take off pretty quickly.

We wrote a number of trading scripts, I should give David most of the credit, to be fair, but these scripts allowed you to move large amounts of coin into and out of both centralized and decentralized exchanges without spooking the market, or making it obvious that you were dumping or hoarding. This was slightly tricky with the decentralized markets because you could get hit with all these transaction fees if you weren't careful. David was our first paid employee. The three of us made a ton of cash, not that we needed it, but we dumped this back into the infrastructure, adding hardware dedicated to decentralized hosting. This turned a slight profit itself, but beyond that was key to making the whole platform hum with efficiency.

SILVA : Please, Mr. Andrews, could you hold on for a second.

ANDREWS : Excuse me?

SILVA : I'm being told that we are being broadcast live on the internet.

ANDREWS : Yeah. That's right.

SILVA : This is a closed hearing. It's not supposed to be livestreamed.

ANDREWS : Not anymore. I'm streaming it.

SILVA : Not anymore, what not anymore?

ANDREWS : It's not anymore a closed hearing. I'm streaming it.

SILVA : Mr. Chairman?

ANDREWS : I want people to hear what I have to say. I won't continue without the livestream. You'll want to hear what I have to say. You don't have to divulge any classified information - you're just asking the questions. Continue?

CHAIR : OK. Continue.

ANDREWS : We were already near billionaires by now, each of the founders having kept some of the what's now called Classic Tapcoin. I was getting tired of Scott's antics also about this time, and had started to go back to school to try and finish my degree, and David was pretending to grow a conscience or something, rambling on about nuances in ethics and retrenching systemic injustices, turned in to a social justice warrior, completely beyond the pale. In fact, he even went out changed genders just to prove a point. I guess we call him Zara, now? OK. Scott on the other hand is a megalomaniac who's completely tone deaf when it comes to anything other than computers, money, and maybe, more money. I couldn't stand to be in the executive board with him - so I told him and David that I was going to buy an island and hang out there the rest of my life, and so to do this I was going to sell my 80% stake.

SILVA : And this is when you got into contact with a Chinese national who goes by Jing. Correct?

ANDREWS : In a manner of speaking, yes. Funny story though. I wanted to keep trading and keep in the crypto scene, but didn't like doing it from my own person and I didn't like Scott and David and some of the losers that hung out with them and were always fawning for their attention. But I do like the crypto scene and the Tapboard we created. I really appreciate the ability to not only be anonymous but multinonymous. You can explore different people. A lot of us well-adjusted human people like to pretend we aren't full of contradictions and have this consistent inner monologue, and society expects people to behave with some consistency. But this forced conformity or nonconformity doesn't allow us to explore all the people we are, or could be, or often, the people we most definitely are not. I hate being pigeonholed. I've always hated it. I've been pigeonholed since preschool. Pigeonholing is the worst. I watched it happen to David. He had some conflicted feelings about life, like oh my god sometimes things aren't black and white, and somehow let people tell him that his problem was that he was a woman. I could maybe agree that he wasn't the frat bro that some people tried to label him, but he never was a woman, until all of these social justice warriors convinced him that he was a woman and the next day he's like "Hi I'm Sara". He was my best friend and I tried to tell him, no, you're not, you're just confused, you can be many people, be who you are, you know, you don't have pigeonhole yourself into one hole just because you don't like the one they put you in. But society doesn't accept this. I'm not gay or nothing, but I really liked David and feel like I lost my best friend to this crap.

So as for me, I discovered that I really like the use of online forums because I can wake up one day and play a different role, try out new ideas, be new people, and see which ones resonate without fear of judgment or social repercussions or anyone telling me I'm doing it wrong. Now, as I mentioned, I had dropped out of college, sort of, my sophomore year. But after making a good amount of money I wanted to go back and finish some courses and finish my degree. Maybe even go on to grad school. I wanted to go into sociology. People fascinate me. Systems fascinate me. I understand people and I understand systems. I've always known I can make contributions. But when I was younger, I made the mistake of getting in debates with people about how I see the world, and they always told me I was wrong,. I was hoping to get some actual academic cred, a degree, maybe eventually a Ph.D. I did some online courses through my liberal arts university, but I really was excited to do my thesis work - independent research. I had struck upon an idea a few years back and wanted to explore it, so I started gathering data. For several years I attended hundreds of online video meetings, like many of us did and I had huge storage space available to me, so I archived all the video data. I decided to test a theory. My theory is that while everybody is racist, the people who claim to be the least racist are actually the most racist. Same for sexism. Well, well, how can you make such a claim? I see you looking at me like how can you test such a claim? Machine learning. Natural Language Processing. These fields were quite advanced already, like I could just plug video into the programs and it transcribes it and then spits out variables describing the sentence structure. The sentence structure changes when people are talking to women or people of color. Not just a little bit, but drastically, night and day. The vocabulary changes. There's dozens of variables that change. You can actually infer the race and gender of someone that is being spoken to, without knowing the person, with like 90% accuracy. This is just applying techniques they've used in other disciplines - for example you can diagnose people with mental illness by analyzing their sentence structure, you know by classifying different phrases and using a bunch of NLP tools, you can chart the language and see very distinct changes when they're addressing a woman or a person of color. This is the worst among those obnoxious white liberals who claim to be anti-racists. They're the worst racists of them all. Without a doubt. I have the data to prove this.

Anyways I tried to put this together and reached out to a thesis advisor and they weren't having it. First they tried nitpicking the science, muttering about all these different sampling specifications and how this wasn't science it was pseudoscience and how 90% isn't an impressive benchmark for this sort of task, and wondering what my ax to grind was - but I don't know I probably have a better understanding of statistics than the median sociology professor, so I didn't back down -

SILVA : Well, if I may, certainly you should have been made aware about the
restrictions on research with human subjects who haven't agreed to be
studied. No thesis advisor is going to sign on to -

ANDREWS : OK so there we go. Exactly. Case in point. This was one of the
nitpicks I heard, exactly, that I had done this "unethically." That kind of
stuff. Here I thought I had found something interesting and everybody is
sitting around arguing about whether they're going to be discountenanced
in their little academic community because this student in their department didn't get informed consent to study their responses in a video chat.
Who cares how I obtained the data or whatever informed consent amounts
to. Truth is truth even if it's inconvenient or obtained without informed
consent. So I never got to publish it. I never graduated - basically the
chair of the sociology department called me in and said that he wouldn't
sign my degree because he believes I am not a true scientist and simply
on a mission to troll people. I think his words were "you are not the type
of person who graduates with a sociology degree from this department."
Needless to say, I was done with my academic dreams at this point. Academics aren't interested in intellectual pursuits, they're only interested in
gatekeeping their tiny, weird little, stupid little fruitless gardens. Not for
me. All these rules regarding research on human subject are nothing but
a gatekeeper's dream. In order to successfully do a study in sociology with
people, you have to basically have a grant, have millions of dollars, enough
to implement all the compliance, and then like 7 years, and you have to get
all the politically correct muckety-mucks all the way up to sign off, there's
this IRB you have to impress, and they're not going for it unless you are
furthering whatever narrative is being pushed at the time, and then by this
time you have like 39 subjects and this isn't really enough to say anything
meaningful. So much gatekeeping. But I wanted to continue intellectual
pursuits, without having to beg permission from the gatekeepers. I like
to think freely without fear of stepping on people's toes. I found this was
easy to do in forums where I didn't have to identify myself. I couldn't
get railroaded out of town this way for saying something politically in-
correct. Our institutions are politically correct to point of dysfunctional
corruption. I once brought up eugenics in an ethics class. You'd think, if

anywhere in the world you could bring up eugenics, and deal with it appropriately, it would be a fucking ethics class. I was told "nah dude that's too edgy let's steer clear." I asked them to define eugenics and everybody refused to even define it. What's the point of higher education if you can't even attempt to define the things you claim to be against? I have a lot of thoughts, I have a lot to say, as you can probably tell. Maybe not all my thoughts are brilliant, but I'm smart enough to sort out the wheat from the chaff with a little honest discussion. As iron sharpens iron, so one man sharpens another.

So I dived into online communities where free speech was permitted and celebrated. I found that while there's more free speech in anonymous forums with no trigger-warnings and PC gatekeepers, it's not a utopia. The problem, after all, is people and the way people process discussion. There's always a pecking order. True free speech is a unicorn. If you are literally nobody, people don't care what you have to say. Free speech is about power. People hold positions of power, like university professors, like the editors of mainstream media, people hold these positions so they can gate-keep. You have to be somehow higher up the chain if you actually want to compete. I remember getting furious when I tried to argue with supposedly more important people online through pseudonyms - none of what I said ever gained any traction against someone more regarded as an authority. Like Scott, for example, he likes to talk and make all these really incredibly stupid little pithy general proverbs that often involve variables X and Y, like you know "The people most likely to claim X blah blah blah" and everybody responds like "ah dude that is sooo deep." I tried to argue with him, offer well-grounded counterexamples, and I'd get 100's of replies screaming that "you know you're conflating correlation with causation" or some of the 6 logical errors that all of the sycophant toe-sucking tools on the internet accuse you of when they don't actually have the capacity to process what you're suggesting. I observed this everywhere, people always acquiesce, even in supposedly honest discussions, they always acquiesce to those higher up the pecking order. It's craven and annoying.

But I guess this is human nature. Humans always seek out the pecking order and believe accordingly. True rational thought is not in our DNA.

Yet I wanted a venue to explore ideas. Like actually have an honest discussion. I'm not this far-right guy. People labeled me as alt-right back then but I was just exploring. Always these people with the labels. I explored communism, fascism, Marxism, all this -isms, you name it. You can't call yourself an anti-fascist unless you have an appreciation for fascism. Sorry to be the one to tell you, but there's a small difference between killing 6 million people based on their genetic heritage they were born with and you know, gender pronoun related micro-aggression. In order to explore these ideas you have to advocate for them, and it helps if you create someone who can not only be someone to whom people listen, but someone you can throw all your intellectual energy into from time to time, you know, take these ideas for a test drive, see if they fit you. My goal was to try out all these ideologies, each from personae that had enough gravity to be taken seriously. You can't just express your ideas anonymously, you have to be someone in order for these ideas to be taken seriously. And if you're skeptical of this, name one cultural guru, influencer who is anonymous, or who wasn't an author, or CEO, or politician, or quarterback, or went to Princeton, and who you pay attention to. You'd think that after 40 years the internet would've produced one. No one has become anybody based on their opinions being regarded as interesting, it's always the other way around. You read an editorial in the New York Times and you say "oh this guy has a Nobel prize in economics" and you take them seriously. When some stupid coked out washed up actor jabs at the president and it agrees with your ideology, you like that and you say "wow you really hit the nail on the head" but in reality 500,000 people were probably thinking the same thing, but you don't care because if the librarian says it you're just like "oh this librarian doesn't she thinks she's clever." I wanted to have a chance to explore different viewpoints in a credible way. As James Andrews, founder of Tapboard, I was slapped with a label and detested by some people but also revered by other people, so I was not someone who was in a position to engage in the discussions I wanted to engage in.

Are you still with me?

SILVA : You are being cryptic.

ANDREWS : Aye, aye. Captain Obvious.

SILVA : So you took the proceeds and tried to create a new persona?

ANDREWS : I sold my shares to "Jing."

SILVA : Oh. I see. But Da, you sold the remainder of your shares to Da. Correct?

ANDREWS : There always has to be two, you know, the yin and the yang. You can't explore one side of an issue without understanding the polar opposite. So it was necessary that I save some shares for Da. Da means "great" in Chinese. Easy symbol to draw, too.

SILVA : Paul Preston described his meeting with Da in great detail.

ANDREWS : I read that on the transcript. "Great" detail. So hilarious.

SILVA : What's hilarious?

ANDREWS : Embellisher's gonna embellish. Useful idiot. Chicago Bulls parka? I was rolling on the floor laughing when I read that. I mean, who's going to make that up? Who's going to make up "Chicago Bulls parka"? Certainly nobody would ever make something like that up, right? that's just soooo random! And believable! We trust you Paul, because you're the only person who has ever met Da. Paul Preston, whisperer to the Great Da.

SILVA : I'm sorry - You read this, You have a transcript? This is a closed hearing.

ANDREWS : Like I said, not anymore.

SILVA : How do you have a transcript?

ANDREWS : I found they were easy to buy, for the right price. Bounties, right? I don't know which one of you gave me the transcripts, but thanks, and I hope you enjoy your ten million dollars. That's probably a large drop in your bucket, but it's an ever smaller drop out of my bucket.

CHAIR : Perhaps you should get to your point sooner rather than later. I can hold you in contempt.

ANDREWS : I'll continue with my story without interruptions. Contempt charges don't really intimidate me. Everyone thought I was gone, but now I was free to operate and do whatever I want. I still owned a large cluster of hardware that ran a portion of the network, and that's when I really got my lucky break: While we have always suggested our clients use TOR and other precautions for accessing decentralized networks, some don't. We don't have a God's view but we can see what's happening on our servers - it turns out we notice we're getting a lot of pings from Capitol Hill IP addresses, and lo and behold it seems like these are corresponding to meeting with the, wait, Senate Intelligence Committee, and it also seems like someone's making some major trades. I didn't know who this was, but I was able to pair the account to other devices and discovered they - he, she, were using some of our scripts to buy and often dump real heavy loads of coins. Some of the scripts that David had written, that is. So I sat back and waited, and then did some leveraged front-running. When I say, I, I mean mostly Jing, sometimes Da. This is why everybody believed that Jing was connected to the Communist Party - they could see Jing making these heavy plays and they assumed, naturally, he was acting on real insider information, which he was, it just wasn't coming from China. Actually I made one of my biggest steps forward in total value when Tapcoin jumped through, or I should say, was shepherded through, averting certain regulatory hurdles. Some of you know what I'm talking about, because you bought a lot of Alice prior to announcements. I could see that and I bought more. Did anyone else think it was a miracle that after years of dealing with impassable regulatory issues, suddenly they all started to fall like dominoes? Really. There are people in this room who made a ton of money speculating, or I guess you can't call it speculating if you know precisely what's going to happen because you're in the room where the regulatory decisions are made, but suffice to say that regulators got paid quite well when Tapcoin was approved. So did I. Do you all realize how unlikely it was that a stablecoin would ever have $15 Trillion marketcap, say 10 years ago? It was a regulatory impossibility. Completely impossible. Major projects would try and ended up shutdown. You've never heard of some of them, but there was a major push, it was a bunch of Princeton kids and hedge fund, they laid the groundwork, but shutdown operations because the amount of regulatory red tape was formidable. All the assets that are needed to form a stablecoin are treated as worst-case scenario for taxes and regulation. Ten years ago the financial engineers figured this out and gave up. It would have been a total nightmare. Until we greased the wheels.

You see, leveraged front-running was good for a while, but I decided why not be proactive? The regulators in charge don't know anything, the regulators with knowledge have no power. This seems like an opportunity. Lobbying is easy if you have money. I see Senator Shelli is on the committee. As some of you know, she operates a hedge fund. Her and her husband Simon. A very very successful one. To be fair, it seemed like it was successful before she was senator, but since she's become senator the returns on her funds have been, for lack of a better word, unbelievable. I knew years back she had several funds that were betting heavy on various crypto-trading strategies. I started offering some advice here and there - buy X, sell Y. I was correct most of the time because I'm good at that thing, and I'm usually right, but the other 20% I have enough weight to move the market. After communicating with the fund manager for a while, I asked for a position on the board. It was a weird ask, because nobody had met me, I did this all remotely under a made-up name. But because I had made 97 out of 100 calls correctly, the manager let me join the board. I became an advisor to Shelli and Simon. I advised to get in early on Alice, as the word in the community was that for security, bandwidth, and regulatory concerns, Alice would be the natural platform on which to build a stablecoin. Then I let them know our goal - promote regulators that would allow a stablecoin. That's where Shelli came in - she worked her magic and made certain the nominations of stablecoin friendly cabinet members and Fed chair. This was really a remarkable transformation in about 18 months - slow enough so that no one noticed, but historically speaking, this was a flash. We went from resigned to the fact that the everyday stablecoin used by everybody would remain eternally elusive, to billions of dollars of ecommerce happening the day Tapcoin went live. And no laws were broken - Shelli might be shy to say how she collaborated with an anonymous advisor, but that's how her crypto funds have averaged 500% annualized returns over a five year period in the middle of the decade.

But the United States is crumbling. It has been for decades. We all know this. We've reached our zenith and have only our nadir to look forward to. Corruption is everywhere. It's the law of the land. We're all just grabbing our chunk before the whole thing collapses. We claim to be a nation of solid values, but a tree is known by it's fruit. I'll get back to this in a minute, but we were talking about our friend Jing. Yes, China, they didn't know who Jing was, and they didn't like this - they like control as much as anybody. Everybody thought Jing was Communist Party and trading on insider intelligence, but not so, so China decided to retaliate against Jing by censoring transactions. Teach Jing a lesson I guess. I had stored quite a bit of my long-term holding in Bitcoin, and people knew more or less what Jing's addresses were, so all of the Chinese mining operations were told that they weren't going to mine on any blocks containing transactions from my addresses. Super annoying. And successful - it turns out it's easy to modify most of the mining software to censor transactions. This was, to my knowledge, the first major censorship operation. Now they do it all the time. But doing it to Jing showed that it worked. The US won't admit that they helped China censor transactions - they want you to believe they only censor transactions of Sudanese terrorists who rape 7 year old girls, not Chinese dissidents. Which, at the time that's basically who Jing was, not even by what he was saying but by who he wasn't. Even though China didn't have a majority of hashing power, just the fact that there was a positive probability that the block would get orphaned, this led most miners throughout the world to blacklist my address. This was before the mining software was using AI for basic optimization and risk minimization. The algorithms didn't know to drop my transactions when I included a fee. This was annoying. I had to include a fee roughly equivalent to the block reward, but also include fees to the next several blocks in order to finalize the transaction. The funny thing is, this didn't convince anybody that Jing wasn't Chinese. Now I actually got lucky with the timing - when I was deciding what to do, Bitcoin spiked quite a bit, thank you Drip Drop, so I had about $100 Billion in Bitcoin. Wonderful. At this point, after some effort I was able to move this out of Bitcoin and after some tumbling took stakes in most chains throughout the world. In particular, as you heard, I was (via Da and "Joey") set up to make a ton of money when Bitcoin coin crashed and Alice shot up, and then the stablecoin went from an utter impossibility to live. By now I owned quite a bit of Alice, and due to being the majority stakeholder of XXY, I'm able to collect rent on nearly all of the international supply chain settlements that happen on the Alice blockchain. By the way I should mention that the team behind the codebase are 100% legit. I couldn't write all that fantastic code myself. These guys are brilliant programmers, the best I could find. They all retired quite wealthy.

I spent the last five years extorting chains throughout the world, seeking and collecting rent, waiting for this very moment. I control significant shares in many of the self-governing protocols throughout the world and extract rent this way - while I don't typically have a majority of shares in anything, it turns out a plurality will get you a long ways if you know how to play the governance game. Speaking of the governance game. Look at you guys. Meeting secretly in the basement of the Senate after a national election was postponed because a bomb went off in the basement of a church. Way to work. Scott owns you all. Do any of you not own Tapboard? I figured as much. That's why you refused to press him on how Tapboard basically made this whole thing possible. Scott is a rich guy and you treat him like your master. But I'm wealthier. I sat down last night and tried to come up with a rough estimate $7.3 Trillion give or take few billion. Easily richest person in history - still more than twice Scott who's worth about $3.5 Trillion. And I still live in my parents basement in Virginia. I rarely visit my island, not sure why I ever bought the damned thing. So that concludes the biographical portion of my statement. Questions?

SILVA : Perhaps you know what these hearings are about - you claim to have obtained a transcript. You seem to indicate that you are in fact behind Da and Jing, and we have suspicions that Da or Jing are likely behind the

recent attacks on election integrity. Are you saying that you are behind
these attacks?

ANDREWS : 'Attack' has unclear connotation. Exploits? Anyways I do have
an answer. I prepared an answer for this, anticipating this moment. Hold
on. So to begin, I should say, I deliberated quite a bit in writing this,
asking myself how to present this. Manifestos are awkward as fuck. You
can't come off reading someone's manifesto and not thinking that person
is batshit crazy and out of touch. Most of them, the manifestos that is,
get ignored, you know - you see this picture of this crazy person with
crazy hair in a mug shot and then you hear so-and-so wrote a 1300 page
manifesto, and you're like "Oh God" and nobody reads them. Seriously
do they have a make-up artist come in and frazzle and grease the suspect's
hair before they take the mugshot? Now I've been writing one for quite a
while, but I realized that the classic method of delivery is horrible. At this
point, I haven't been caught committing or attempting a crime, I know
I'm a suspect at this point, but at the moment I have all of your attention,
despite the fact that I haven't blown anything up or shot up a school.

But here we are now - most of you don't know me, but you can see I'm
a person, I have facial expressions, emotions, nuance. I have a lot going
on. I even have a sense of humor. I'm not some mugshot. Also, I should
mention that I resisted even using the term "manifesto" for awhile because
it's so basic, so cliché, but I decided the shock value was worth it. I'm
not going to actually present a manifesto. I'm just going to talk, and the
entire world is going to hear me, because everybody by now wants to know
what I have to say. Wanting people to listen, you can't just tap them on
the shoulder you have to at least threaten them with a sledgehammer, and
then you'll notice you have their strict attention.

To begin, I should say that I've been a student of sociology and anthro-
pology, not at a university, but from my vantage point as a technological
master of the universe. I know things now. Two things in particular. First
of all, everybody, every single person who has lived or will live, everyone
in this room, myself, others, we are all what commonly goes by the term
'racist'. It's biological. If given a choice, you would throw others to the

wild beasts to save your own kin. Liberals make great efforts to cover this up, to hide this, to apologize for this ugly truth when it creeps out, or to blame other people for it, but this is the truth. Second, the world is small, and there are simply not enough resources for all of us. Thus it is logical and inevitable: There will be a race war. There are no better angels of our nature to save us, there are only genes that are the most fit.

But I shouldn't say that there will be a race war, when the race war has in fact already begun. We are being replaced, encroached upon and are breeding with immigrants. The majority of Europeans in The United States of America is under threat and this majority will be vanishing in the next few years. Mass immigration and the higher fertility rates of the immigrants themselves threaten the balance here in the US. We are experiencing an invasion on a level never seen before in history. Millions of people pouring across our borders, legally, invited by the state and corporate entities. Beyond this direct invasion, we are seeing a slow genocide by interbreeding, in a sense. Due to mass immigration we lack the time scale we need to return to health and prosperity. Mass immigration will disenfranchise us, subvert our nations, destroy our communities and our culture. Mass immigration is the first step in a bloodless war to destroy us.

Now I'm going to pause for a second, and make a point, I should be clear, as I know one question I'm going to hear is "are you a white supremacist? Oh my God you sound like a white supremacist." My answer to that question is "what does that even mean?' What does it mean to claim that one race is superior to another? Do you eat an orange and declare that oranges are superior to apples? Are you forced to ask whether dogs are "superior" to cats. I'm a cat man myself. That doesn't mean I'm a cat supremacist. I just like cats and don't like dogs. If you like dogs, good for you. Just keep them out of my house. So my answer to the inevitable and predictable question "are you a white supremacist?" is "why are you asking these sort of questions, why does everything have to come with judgment or supremacy or non-supremacy?" I'm white. I like white people. I like black people too, not all of them, but I'm white. I certainly don't like every white person either. Stop asking stupid questions and imposing your own ideas of moral judgments on other people. I should also say that while I'm saying there is going to be a race war, if Africa or Asia wins, good for them, they're entitled to the spoils. I won't begrudge that. So I'm not literally a white supremacist until we've won the race war, in which case we will all have to be white supremacists, by the tautology of the proposition. It's not like dinosaurs are inferior, they're just not fit, based on the tautological definition that fit means you're not dead. But while we're on the subject of white supremacists, who do you think are the real white supremacists? The paternalistic so-called liberals and progressives, who are so determined they have to help an entire race because that race can't help themselves? That sounds about as paternalistic as it gets. But, of course, they don't actually want to help. And this applies to all of you sitting there in congress, you make laws that you want to look like you're making some effort, but it's all theater. Just admit it, you're all white supremacists. The way you discuss things like reparations is so sickeningly paternalistic.

But listen, I know you all want to label me as something, in order to fit your narrow minds you have to label me with some sort of -ism. Like I said I'm not a white supremacist, but I know you're going to label me as that, so just to fill that void, you can go ahead and call me an accelerationist. You might have to look that up, but I'd prefer that when you talk about me over the next few days and you need some adjective to describe some sort of ideological box you'd like to toss me in, and I know you will do this, can we just go with accelerationist? Great. I'm an accelerationist.

Now the race war, at least the violent part, might not happen today, tomorrow, or even this generation. But it will happen. And before it happens each race should retreat to their own shores, to their own people, and not accept the weakening of their race by interbreeding.

SILVA : I'm going to have to stop you there. This is beyond offensive. Get to your point very soon.

ANDREWS : See. You're making my point. You're "going to have to stop" me because I said something offensive. What if this is what I think? Can I say what I've come to in my own mind after years of thoughts and observation?

Don't you think it's a bit discriminatory to crack down on my free speech when I'm speaking my mind? The hypocrisy. But whatever, in the end it's very simple. In the end I don't need to convince you to go along with my reasons - I have leverage. So perhaps we fast forward to the demands portion of our discussion. Perhaps that's a better plan. If you're getting all freaked out about the interbreeding stuff, I'm sure you won't like what else I have to say. That's fine. We have plenty of time to get to know each other and come to more of an understanding.

I suppose before I tell you what I want. Perhaps I should tell you a little bit more about what I have.

SILVA : Stop pontificating here. Tell us what you want to tell us and quit jerking yourself off.

ANDREWS : Oooh. Getting a bit ruffled, are we? Good for you. As you may have gathered by now, I own majority stake in the largest decentralized future, commodities, and supply chain settlement network. The settlement network itself is where billions of dollars of funds are settled everyday. If something goes awry with the protocol, thousands of businesses, farms, producers, distributors, consumers, don't get paid. I hold trillions in Tapcoin in hundreds of thousands of accounts. If you don't believe me, I can demonstrate this to anyone who understands cryptography: I'm sharing a list of 100,000 hashed accounts. Got it? Now pick any of them I will unhash them with my private key - you can verify this with my public key provided at the top the document. Then I will move these accounts. Any takers? Pick a hash. Pick a random number? That's fine. You all trust me. Or perhaps you don't understand how a cryptographic proof works.

I also think a few remarks are in order with regards to the house of cards that you've created. Look at the economy. Remember when they said never to let the national debt get near the GDP? We're now well beyond that. And you can't figure out how to collect taxes - is this because y'all are rich and self-serving or just corrupt and self-serving, or is it maybe both? Or maybe you really believe that you can outrun every economic downturn by printing money. How is this working out? Oh yes, it's great for you guys in the Senate - average wealth is $8 billion. Of course this is slightly misleading- the median wealth of a US senator is only $180 million. And I understand most of you own cryptocurrencies and have profited greatly over the last 6-8 years. I'm not going to go accusing you of insider trading, but, yeah, well, it looks pretty much like insider trading. Do you know that the median US taxpayer has a net worth of negative $80,000? There are hundreds of counties in the Midwest where the sum net worth of all residents is negative - that means all of the land, houses, assets, businesses, individual wealth, add this all up and it's smaller than the debt held out of state. Did you know that Tapboard takes a cut of 40% of the world's transactions? Thanks to TapTurk, approximately 30% of the country is earning in 12 hour days what would have been minimum wage 8 hour days 15 years ago. All to payoff their debts. Oh, but you say, they aren't poor, they have TapPhones and hybrid cars and enjoy all the modern conveniences, and sweet AR gaming systems, so no, they're not poor. But c'mon, they're spending 12 hours a day on their TapPhones doing tasks and delivering products and running errands in their nice cars, which are required for most of the deliveries. If you think the economy is a delicate, inflated bubble that needs constant stimulus, don't think too hard about the whole socio-economic political situation: it's a tinderkeg. Both wealth and and income equality are higher than in the French revolution, or the Bolshevik revolution. Every boom bust cycle it grows worse. The next cycle might be the last. If the bubble starts to deflate, the lowest will take the hit first, but this time it won't be the bottom 10% who really get screwed, it will be the bottom 70%, who really really get screwed, and they won't be happy. Good luck justifying your median $180 Million existence when that shit hits the fan. They say you have to keep dancing as the long as the music keeps playing, and that's what you do for sure, but they never tell you what to do if the music stops.

So to summarize: We have an overinflated asset bubble, the highest wealth inequality in history, more than half of employment in the temporary or gig work category, and about 70% of transactions happening on blockchains.

What could possibly go wrong?

I have a plan to fix some of this. You aren't going to like it. It involves some fiscal responsibility and will necessarily redress some of your largesse. But it will bring us back on track. You'll hear about this plan soon enough.

I own a significant stake in each of the top 25 cryptocurrencies. Selling my stake in any of these would crash the market. But I'm more clever than that - I wouldn't want to just crash the market, I'm more interested in picking winners and losers. Not just in the crypto-currency sphere but in the geopolitical sphere - I have a long list of addresses belonging to the People's Coin Treasury of North Korea, and many other foes of the United States. Considering the GDP of North Korea is like $50 Billion, I'm sure their supreme leader would be eager to see what they could do with $1 Trillion in cryptocurrency.

I own real estate in over 150 countries, about $500 Billion worth. Some of this is speculative, but much of it I collect rent on. Millions of people live on my land. They pay rent to me, but they don't know that. They think they're paying rent to whatever-the-fuck holdings LLC. These are all shell companies that literally exist part on a blockchain and the rest in a folder somewhere in Wyoming. I can redistribute the property however I see fit. Or I can literally evict them from their houses through a smart contract, and lock them out. Or I could give their property to Iran, China, or North Korea or some meth-head in Idaho.

I should also tell you about my fault tolerant executor network. I appreciate how Paul gave you an introduction to the concept of executor network. I have appointed over 20,000 accounts, some smart contracts, that run on dozens of blockchains throughout the world, using their own interoperability protocol.

SILVA : Mr Chairman. Can I yield my time and motion for a recess?

CHAIR : Mr Andrews, you have 3 minutes. Tell us what you want.

ANDREWS : You've given no time restrictions on the witnesses.

CHAIR : Without objections I'm limiting Mr. Andrew's remaining statement to 3 minutes

GOLDING : Objection.

CHAIR : Dear Lord. OK. Please continue and arrive at your point, please, Mr. Andrews.

ANDREWS : James. Please. I insist. As I was saying. And by the way, were I ever to be say, Speaker of the House, I would have a much manlier gavel. That thing is flaccid. Anyways. These accounts assure my safety and assure that if my safety is ever compromised, my desires will be fulfilled. Beyond that, this network allows me to write a sort of decentralized program that will execute in my absence, in response to real-world events. Each node on this network has very simple instructions - to send out certain types of transaction in certain situations. If I'm ever threatened, these nodes have instructions on what transactions to broadcast, and these instructions are incentivized. If the nodes tell the truth and do it promptly, their reward is lucrative. If they fail to broadcast the correct transaction, or worse, if they broadcast the wrong transaction, heaven forbid, they lose their stake and are kicked off the network. I've taken pains to make this network properly decentralized and deeply robust. The actors are anonymous, but I'm quite confident they are decentralized. By the way, this method of using the crowd as an oracle is well-tested. Truth is the ultimate Schelling Point. Tell the truth, get the reward, attempt to lie, you lose your stake. Now the network per se doesn't know truth from falsehood, but again Truth is the only Schelling point, and it would take an exceeding improbable rejection of human psychology and game theory to collectively choose a falsehood even if it led to a more socially acceptable outcome. It's the prisoner's dilemma at play. Perhaps I'm losing some of you with the terminology, so I will be blunt. If I am to be arrested, there are thousands of nodes that are supposed to broadcast certain transactions. Other nodes, most of which are automated by smart contracts I have running, are waiting to process these transactions, including rewarding the correct answers, and also unleashing whatever action I have specified. For example, to begin, I've programmed, if you will, this network, so that if I am arrested, I will transfer 2 Trillion to the treasury of North Korea. You don't want that. Now there's a few questions you have obviously - how do these people all know who I am considering I've been known to absolutely no one for quite some time? That's a good question, and the answer is

- Easy. In the document I just shared, I included a hashed confirmation. All of the nodes that have confirmed this get $20,000 each, and it looks like most have. So now that my identity is publicly known, all of the nodes are active and are watching me. Most at least. I don't need all, but most, those that want to be paid. And thankfully for me, in this planet of 10 billion people, there's a lot of people that need money to feed themselves and their family. You might ask again, how do I verify this? Again, great question. I'm sharing a new document, giving thousands of hashes and a rough and splotchy map of the network. This is a little bit more for the experts, I apologize, but if you pick a number I can uncover how a certain piece of psuedocode is executed on my network. Of course I'm not giving you the whole network, as then authorities could isolate each node. But the network is fault tolerant enough that I can sacrifice a few nodes here and there if any of you would like some convincing. Another reason I'm not sharing the entire network is that this would facilitate the network communicating directly with each other. At this point they can't. They only can follow instructions or not follow instructions. The smart contracts take care of the in-between interactions. No takers? Again you trust me. Very good.

SILVA : I'm sorry this document appears like nonsense to me.

ANDREWS : Of course it does. Maybe you know someone with a science degree who can explain it to you?

SILVA : Stop wasting our time. What do you want?

ANDREWS : I'm sending you one more document. If the demands are satisfied, the network verifies this, and the appropriate action is executed by the network. If the demands are not satisfied, my network generates a 'FAIL' code and the unpleasant alternative is executed. We go to the "disagreement point" of Nash that Scott referred to. I can't stop it - there's no way for me to change it without spending weeks or months reincentivizing the network one contract at a time. So my demands are important and my threats are credible. I will get what I want. I challenge everybody to contact their friends who do cryptography and their friends who program smart contracts. It all checks out. You have some time. In fact you have until next Tuesday.

SILVA : Tuesday?

ANDREWS : You have this document?

SILVA : You just sent a list of congressional districts and a name for each.

ANDREWS : Oh right, here's one for the US Senate, too.

SILVA : What is this list?

ANDREWS : These lists are for everybody. These are the candidates who will win on Tuesday. These are the Real People that Paul and Anna referred to.

SILVA : We can't decide who wins the election, Mr. Andrews. There is absolutely -

ANDREWS : You mean "we" as in the Senate? Of course not! That would be some fucked up version of democracy if the Senate could just choose the winners of the election, obviously that wouldn't be democracy now, would it? And please, I told you, call me James.

SILVA : Then how are you suggesting these candidates will win the election?

ANDREWS : Maybe I should tell you what happens if any one of these candidates loses. If any single one of these candidates is not elected and seated (or if I'm arrested or prosecuted, or have any freedoms taken away, but this goes without saying, obviously don't fucking heliobeam my island) two unpleasant things will happen. One is that much of the economy will be sent into shock when much of the blockchain gets decimated when the economic doomsday contracts are activated. Second, I give $2 Trillion to North Korea. They get to choose what they do with that.

Now. How do the odds look?

Wait, you say, but isn't that the wrong side of the race war? Like I said, I'm not really taking sides. I'm using leverage. If we are too stupid, we lose. I'm not going to get in the way of the natural order of things, only accelerate them. We've chosen to embrace a weak and liberal culture were weakness is considered a virtue, especially in leadership. Maybe this is the end of our line.

SILVA : You can't threaten us with disrupting the market if your candidates don't win, I mean you can't be serious.

ANDREWS : As I've mentioned, I have the most developed executor network in history. It's layered with intermediate smart contracts. The beauty is that many of the human nodes don't realize they are nodes, they're just part of a big mechanical turk which pays them well. I have thousand of contracts that are tuned to hundreds of fault-robust state channels keeping track of my demands and my well-being. Once something happens, there are incentives to change the state channels, and so this will happen, in fact there is a sort of a race to change them. The contracts will be activated. There are multiple state channels ready to verify the winner in each of the races. The operators are very much disincentivized from lying. Again it's like a giant prisoner's dilemma and everyone is guilty - the first ones to confess have a chance to go free. What do these poison contracts do? Several things. One, they play games with the consensus - like paying miners to erase chunks of transactions randomly. I have 100,000 poison contracts, ready to be activated. These were really fun to design. They work cross-blockchain. You are incentivized in one asset to destroy blocks from other chains. It will be round-robin cannibalization of most of the blockchain space. I've picked a winner or a few winners, and your job will be to guess that winner. I'll make it clear slowly, who the losers are, and then it will be a prisoner's dilemma situations with everybody racing to defect first. Who will win? Many of these poison contracts will do simple things like pay miners multiples of the block reward to find, mine and reward double spend transactions. What do you do if you're running a business and it turns out each transaction only has an 65% chance of being erased in a few days? It really screws your business model. And if you're someone who likes to try double spends, this is your moment. This will essentially shut down the centralized exchanges. Because I have a majority stake in XXY, these contracts can wreak havoc with the settlement of billions of dollars of supply-chain contracts. There's a costly and rarely used dispute mechanism that escalates and ties up assets. I can trigger this in a way that will freeze most of the contracts. I also have a contract that buys and sell assets on decentralized exchanges. These will work in tandem with the contracts designed to destroy other blockchains. Considering the size of my holdings, this could cause trillions of dollars of value to fall out of markets throughout the world. Were you planning to retire based on your crypto hodlings? Might have to work a few more years.

Then there's the stablecoin. Tapcoin. Yes, You all have some. There's $15 Trillion in circulation. I've been messing with the security parameters, as Scott described. He's correct. 100%. The security parameters are really really weak. I own a significant portion of the bonds. I should be honest, I can't be 100% confident that I can crash the whole thing. In fact, if I were to bet I would say 95%. But the security parameters are really weak. There's a chance that $15 trillion will be wiped off the face of the earth. Why the uncertainty? It depends largely on people's behavior collectively. We know this is hard to predict. When markets start crashing, all of a sudden if you're holding one of these bonds, you have to ask yourself which blockchain is it settled on? What is it denominated in? Is your exchange going to be liquid or are they going to be vulnerable to a run? I've used human greed and polarization to hammer away at the security parameters to the point where the security is almost non-existent. There are so many derivative products that involve these bonds, it's hard to say how liquid they will be or how badly the crash will leak into other markets. It's unclear what rational behavior will be, because everybody will be looking at each other trying to guess not only who's going to run for the door first, but what or where exactly is the door? Remember the Suckening? That took like 18 months. The Unsuckening will take like 18 hours. As Scott mentioned, you'd have approximately $2.5 Trillion worth of government paper dumped onto financial markets pretty much overnight.

Now I've posted a few details - many of these are quite technical, if you are well-versed in smart contracts you can read this. I'm leaving this to the experts to parse and explain to the general public exactly the ramifications.

You have 'til Tuesday.

SILVA : Can't we just censor the transactions?

ANDREWS : Very good question. It seems like you've learned something this week. You don't know all the nodes ahead of time until it's too late. There's too many. Also, many of the contracts are legitimate, performing mundane DeFi operations on the side. If you shut these down you end up shutting down much of the functioning network. It would take months to go through and censor enough transactions to have an effect. You could try pausing the entire global financial system for a while, but you would have to do this repeatedly as each epoch more nodes will reveal themselves. And all the censorship mechanisms require incentives that you can't provide. So, good luck with that, I'm glad you're thinking pro-actively.

So. I think it's clear. Elect these gentlemen Tuesday and everything will be fine, everything will be alright. Don't, and you can expect the biggest major global financial meltdown in history and as a bonus you can welcome North Korea as one of the major financial players in the New World Order. I'm sure they will be delightful. Also I should mention, you'll find some other easter eggs in the contract, if these gentleman are elected, I will be donating $1 trillion to the US treasury, for the purpose of getting the upper hand on the national debt. A drop in the bucket, yes, but, I'm sure the gentleman I've chosen are going to pay attention to the national debt this time.

But I don't think there are going to be any issues. As I mentioned before, debate depends much more on power and pecking order than one would naively like to believe. I think you will all find that my ideas are much closer to the truth, when you understand that I have the power. People are like that, it's an adaptive trait. Perhaps some of you think my ideas are not very palatable today, they make as much sense to you as saying that two plus two makes five. But, I trust that by Tuesday, you will find my ideas will be much more compelling, and will have been presented widely and with much more gusto and grace than I humbly offer to you today. In the end, it will be favorable to believe that the men I've chosen to lead the country will do an admirable job, considering the risk of believing that they will not.

SILVA : It seems as if - Mr. Andrews?

CHAIR : It appears as if the witness has ended the session. I'm calling a recess
to consider the recent testimony.

9

STATEMENT OF THE FEDERAL RESERVE, JOINT WITH WHITE HOUSE, HOMELAND SECURITY AND DEPARTMENT OF DEFENSE.

For years, we have been monitoring financial markets, including volatile cryptocurrencies, and studying their effects on the domestic and foreign economy. The statements published yesterday may paint a shocking picture to the uninitiated observer. Fortunately, this not a situation that we are unprepared for.

We do not want to take the choice away from Americans, and thus we are not going to tell anybody who to vote for, that is not our position. You should vote for the best candidates, as you would in any other election. Please, do not be influenced by these vacant threats.

After consulting with central banks of Russia, China, India, the European Union and the African Economic Coalition, we have signed today a Memorandum of Understanding that will ensure the economic continuity going forward. The MOU ensures that if any shocks were to hit the cryptocurrency ecosystem, the parties will collectively take custody of every major blockchain, and are prepared to run permissioned networks controlled by the nations in the treaty. Such an arrangement, if necessary, would maintain some of the decentralized spirit, but overall will reduce inefficiencies. We feel it is by now well past the time that nation-states cooperate to create a healthy global economy. Most activity would continue without a hitch, but we can't promise there won't be some frustrating setbacks. If the threats are actualized, there will be some minor disruption while the activity transfers to the permissioned networks. But again, these are but minor issues that will prove to be no more than a mere blip in the trajectory of the global economy.

In the long run, this would be a boon for the global economy. We are prioritizing Tapcoin, as this blockchain has the largest reach. With permissioned servers in every continent verifying transactions, this blockchain will continue to process with lightning speed. Further, because the coalition of national treasuries will control the supply and the development, we have more control over the money supply. This will give us more flexibility in dealing with economic booms and busts. It's unfortunate that the recent events had to cause such an anxious moment for the nation, but we are more hopeful about the longterm stability of global economy than ever before.

Again, we would like to stress to every voter that democracy is intact and healthy as ever. The choice is up to you, as it should be. So this coming Tuesday, we implore you, vote, vote your convictions, vote your conscience, and vote with confidence.

Acknowledgments

The game-of-chicken vulnerability present in ranked-choice voting methods was pointed out to me by Seth Odam during email discussion. Thanks to Sara Wolk for putting me in touch with Seth and facilitating this discussion. Thanks also to David Gerard for email discussions and sending me an early copy of *Libra Shrugged*, which informed some of the narrative.

Printed in Great Britain
by Amazon

23284694R00099